J. J. Kennedy

Desdemona

A Drama in Five Acts

J. J. Kennedy

Desdemona
A Drama in Five Acts

ISBN/EAN: 9783337343262

Printed in Europe, USA, Canada, Australia, Japan

Cover: Foto ©Andreas Hilbeck / pixelio.de

More available books at **www.hansebooks.com**

DESDEMONA,

A

-

Drama in Five Acts,

BY

VERY REV. J. J. KENNEDY,

Rector of St. Mary's Church,

CARROLLTON, MISSOURI.

DESDEMONA.

Introduction.

Desdemona was written to supply a want for an easy, legitimate Drama for the Amateur Societies of the Parish. The Story is founded on facts and told from an American Catholic standpoint. There are no burlesques or depraved Caricatures depicted. On the contrary, we have endeavored to place before your view Characters of Integrity possessing a lofty Patriotism and genuine Christianity.

CARROLLTON, MISSOURI,

FEAST OF ST. MATTHEW SEPTEMBER 21. 1899

DESDEMONA.

CAST OF CHARACTERS.

Mr. Stephen Dawson..............................A Farmer

George Sears .....   — ......Mine Owner

Count LaFar.....................................A French Count

" Mr. Andrew Ready..............................A Farmer

Prof. Barret......................Professor of Music

Syl Blake...Real Estate Man

Sir Albert Murdock...........................English Lord

" Tom Moore.....................................A Mining Clerk

" Andrew Giles.............................Dealer in Mining Stocks

" Jack Deluerty..........................Foreman of Mine

Father Austin.............................Rector of St. Paul's

" Jasper......................................Negro Servant

Master Raymond Barret...................Son of Prof. Barret

Dr. Gross ....Physician

Perkins.......................................Mine Owner

Sergeant Proctor.................................... Soldier

Mrs. Julia Dawson.....................Wife of Stephen Dawson

Miss Desdemona Dawson.....................Daughter of Mr. Dawson

Mrs. Mona Barret...........................Wife of Prof. Barret

Miss Celia Barret..............................Sister of Prof. Barret

Miss Agnes Barret....................Daughter of Prof. Barret

Sister Clare.....................................Hospital Nurse

DESDEMONA----A Drama in Five Acts.

ACT I.—SCENE 1.

Prof. Barret's house, Folger street, Carrollton, Mo. Prof. Barret and Miss Celia Barret, his sister—Miss Barret is singing—the professor is looking over some music—Bell rings—Miss Celia goes to the door.

Celia Barret.   Why, George Sears, I am so glad to see you.   Welcome, Cousin George.

Prof. Barret.   How do you do, my young friend!

George Sears.   I am well, I thank you.

Prof. Barret.   Be seated, George.   When did you arrive from Old Kentucky?

George Sears.   I came last night on the "Q" road about 6:40 and was so tired after supper at the Florence that I went immediately to bed.

Celia Barret.   You look so well, George, but I am surprised that you came that round about way of the "Q" road.   I should much prefer to come on the Wabash, the "Old Reliable" road, from St. Louis.

Sears.   Pardon me, Miss Celia, but I was obliged to come over the "Q" or remain in St. Louis till evening and then take the night train over the Wabash, and not get here till this morning.

Mr. Barret.   Well, it would be even better than to travel over the rough "Q" road.

Sears.   Yes, I grant you all that, but I cannot sleep on the cars at night, and moreover wanted to get here as soon as possible.

Miss Celia.   I am sure we are delighted that you had no accident and reached Carrollton Heights all right.   By the way, how is your mother and all the folks?   Is Miss Betty going to school yet?

Sears.   Yes, mother is very well, indeed; she looks as young and hearty as when you saw her four years ago.   As for Betty she has grown up a young lady.   She will soon be seventeen.   She attends school at Nazareth Academy; mother thinks she will become a Nun.

Celia Barret. What do you think of that, Mr. Sears? Have you any objection to your sister becoming a Nun?

Sears. I should not oppose any serious objection, though I confess I should prefer that she remain in the world and form an alliance with some honorable gentleman. However, Celia, I believe that Almighty God has allotted a particular path for us to follow here on earth.

Celia Barret. I shouldn't like to be a Nun and spend all my days praying and teaching.

Mr. Barret. No danger of you being a Nun. You would rather be somebody's sister. Pardon me, Cousin George, but you have not left Kentucky for good?

Sears. No, not at all, but mother and friends having counseled about me, came to the conclusion that whilst I had not yet got into the swing I had best go West and try my fortune.

[Mrs. Mona Barret enters.]

Mrs. Mona. Well, well, George Sears, I am so glad to see you! Welcome to Carrollton. How are all the folks at home?

George Sears. They are all well and send you their kindest regards.

Mrs. Mona. My! George, how you have grown since we saw you last, four years ago!

Sears. Yes, Mrs. Barret, I have grown considerably, but it is only since I left college that I have developed into a man.

Mr. Barret. Where did you finish you course, George?

Sears: I finished my course at Louisville two years ago. Here is my graduation medal. (All look at it and declare: It is fine, indeed, and you should be proud of it.)

George Sears. Indeed, I am thankful to God for the ability to graduate—moreover I shall hold this medal in dear remembrance of my Alma Mater. Mr. Barret, how are the children?

Mr. Barret. Raymond and Agnes are both well. Mona; tell the children to come in.

(Exit Mona.)

4

Miss Celia. Well, well, Cousin George, your coming is quite a surprise to us all.

[Enter Mona and the children.]

Mona. Mr. Sears, allow me to present our children. This is Raymond, and this is our Agnes. We are proud of them and they are dear good children.

Sears. I am glad to see you, children (taking Agnes on his lap). Agnes, you no doubt can play; if you and Raymond will play for me I shall send you a Christmas present from the Rocky Mountains.

Agnes. Will you send us a bear?

Raymond. I would like an eagle or a buffalo.

Barret. Why, children, those would be rather wild pets. Tell Mr. Sears to send you whatever he thinks best.

Agnes and Raymond: Mr. Sears, do please send us what you think best and we will be glad.

Mona. Children, you may be sure that Cousin George will send you presents that will be useful.

Sears. Yes, children, I shall try and select something good for you. Mr. Barret, do you remember when we visited the Mammoth Cave together?

Mona. What did you do, George, with the specimens you gathered.

Sears: I gave most of them to the college at Louisville for the museum. Mother has the rest. Well, Mr. Barret, you are still teaching music.

Barret. Yes, George, Celia and myself have a good class besides I lead the orchestra at the opera. We have invested some in Railroad Stocks and hope some day to go to Europe and endeavor to get on the top round of the musical ladder.

Mona. Mr. Sears, now the children wish to play for you.

Sears. Yes, I shall be very glad.

Agnes and Raymond, We'll do the best we can. (They play.)

Sears. Now, dear friends, I have had a splendid time and am glad to be with you, but I must be going.

Mr. Barret, Mona and Celia. Where are you going, George?

Agnes and Raymond: Cousin George, do stay with us.

Sears. Yes, dearest, I love you all and prefer to stay with you. But you know I came unannounced and there are two gentlemen at the Florence Hotel whom I wish to consult on some matters.

Barret. Beware, George, and consider well whom you talk to about your business affairs. You know you are entirely welcome and I hope you will consider our house your home whilst you are in the city.

Sears. Yes, Mr. Barret, I shall, but must get all the information I can about the Rockies. There are two gentlemen, Drummers, I believe, at the hotel that have been all through the mountains and have had some years of experience. I want their knowledge and will tarry at the hotel only a day or two. Then I shall return and be at home with you.

Mona and Celia. I trust that you will. Take care of yourself and come up as soon as possible.

Prof. Barret. By the way, George, we are to spend the day in the country to-morrow. I do wish you would go. We'll just have a picnic at Dawson's. I know you will enjoy the company of Desdemona.

Mona and Celia. Yes, by all means come.

Barret. We'll call at Hotel at 9:30.

Sears. Business before pleasure. However, I promise to go if possible. Good night. All, good night.

(Exit George Sears.)

ACT I.—SCENE 2.

Dawson's house—Tress—Croquet grounds. Syl Blake, Prof. Barret, Mona and Celia Barret are discovered playing croquet. The children romp about the grounds and play in the hammock. Mrs. Dawson sitting enjoys the game and the company of the children.

Celia Barret. Mr. Blake, it is your shot now. Strike the professor's ball if possible. (He strikes and misses.)

Mona. It's my turn next. Celia, I'll hit your ball; there I did it.

Mr. Barret. I am for the stake—being a rover I'll help my partner.

[Enter George Sears and Miss Desdemona Dawson.]

Desdemona.   Why, Prof. Barret, you and Mona are ahead.

Syl Blake.   I haven't played for a year——

Desdemona.   It's your turn, now shoot to your partner.

(They play on.)

Desdemona and Mr. Sears walk over and sit in the hammock.

Desdemona.   Well, Mr. Sears, what do you think of Missouri?

Sears.   Well, I of course think there is no place like home However much I admire our Kentucky home I will say that Missouri, as far as I have seen it, is very beautiful.

Desdemona,   Yes, Missouri is a great State and has within its boundaries all, or almost all the productions of Nature.

Sears.   I have no doubt but that Missouri is great Commonwealth.

Desdemona.   Indeed, I think that if our State would be walled in it could get along without the rest of the world.

Sears.   Yes, I do believe that if Kentucky was walled in with Missouri they would most assuredly get along.

Desdemona.   Mr. Sears, what do you mean?

Sears.   I verily believe that Missouri is a good State to live in.

Desdemona.   I am glad that you have a good opinion of our State.

George Sears.   Yes, indeed I have and I have great faith in the United States.   Though a Southerner by birth and education I have learned to love our neighbors of the North.

Desdemona.   Indeed, I am glad to hear it.

(Farm bell rings.)

George Sears.   What is that bell, Miss Dawson?

Desdemona.   It calls the workmen to dinner.   (Both arise and walk about the grounds.   The croquet game is over.)

Mr. Dawson and hands come in from the fields.

Desdemona.   Mr. Sears, this is father.   Father, Mr. Sears from Kentucky.

Dawson.   Glad to see you, young man.

Barret.   How are you to-day, Mr. Dawson?

Dawson. I am well, I thank you.

Mona.   Why, Mr. Dawson, what is that you have in your left hand?

Dawson.   It is only a young rattler that I killed out in the field.

Celia. A snake!   Children, come and see the snake.

Dawson. (Holds it up to view, and hangs it on a tree and says;) Children, come to me and shake hands.   That snake is dead and cannot hurt you.

Agnes and Raymond. We are so glad, Mr. Dawson, it is dead.

Dawson. Come, now, folks, we must all have something to eat.

Desdemona. Yes, we shall. (Exit Dawson into house.)

[Jasper arranges tables on the lawn and all sit down.]

Barret. Who can tell the best business in life?

Celia Barret. I can. To be a United States Senator.

Syl Blake. I think a baker is the best off.

George Sears. I am of opinion that farming is the noblest occupation of man.

Desdemona, Are you a farmer?

Sears. No, Miss Dawson, I am not, though I was reared on the farm.

Desdemona. Excuse me, sir, but do you intend to follow farming as a business?

George Sears. Not at all, Miss Dawson; but from observation and experience I can safely say that the farm is the best home and occupation for man.

Prof. Barret. Why do you consider it so?

George Sears. I am convinced of the fact for many reasons. In the first place there is more pure air in the country. Then it is a better place to develop both mind and body than in the city's throng. Again, there is better company in the country; the trees, plants and flowers and the birds of the air speak to us continually of the Omnipotence of God. Man, moreover, is more sure of a permanency in the country because his capital, the soil, cannot be destroyed.

Desdemona. Then, I presume, that you have come from

Kentucky to select a farm in Missouri?

George Sears. No, Miss Dawson, I have no taste for the soil, and will not engage in farming. I like geology very much and particularly am fond of minerology. In fact, I am a bimetallist and will strike the mountains for my fortune.

Desdemona. Indeed! Are you going West very soon?

George Sears. Yes, Miss Dawson, I intend leaving for the mountains in a few days.

Desdemona. Where do you intend to cast your lot?

George Sears. Indeed I cannot say now.

Mrs. Dawson. Well, Mr. Sears, we would like to hear from you and wish you prosperity in your new business.

George Sears. Thank you! Thank you! I of course will write to my friends.

Desdemona. May we consider ourselves among the number?

George Sears. Certainly, Miss Dawson; and I may be able to gather a few specimens of ore and curios for your cabinet.

Desdemona. I thank you very much.

[Enter Mr. Dawson and Andrew Ready, a neighbor.]

Mr. Dawson. Well, folks, here is Mr. Ready, a good friend of mine and a capital story teller.

Prof, Barret. This is a very warm summer, Mr. Ready.

Andrew Ready. Indade it is barren for those who can always stay in the shade.

Desdemona. Mr. Ready, this is Mr. Sears, a young gentleman from Kentucky. Mr. Sears, Mr. Ready.

Andrew Ready. Ah, indeed! I am glad to mate you, Mr. Sears.

George Sears. Excuse me, sir, but I am not ready to be mated yet a while!

Andrew Ready. I meant no offense, young man, but in Ould Ireland we pronunce the vowels longer than here. I suppose you would say meet, sir?

George Sears. Yes, sir.

Andrew Ready. Well, then I suppose that you'll be a mating some time or other, and sure it's no harum to wish you a good partner for life.

George Sears. No, indeed, Mr. Ready.

Mrs. Dawson. Folks, sit down. (All sit down.)

(Jasper arranges the seats for them and gets food.)

George Sears. I suppose, Mr. Ready, that there is a great contrast between Ireland and America?

Andrew Ready. Yes, sir; there's a great differenc entirely between Ireland and America. Ireland is a very beautiful country, but she is down-trodden in every way be the Laws and Landlords. America is God's own country, where the great Flag of the Republic grants Civil and Religious Liberty to all its citizens who honor it and behave themselves rightly.

Mr. Dawson. What is that you say, Mr. Ready?

Andrew Ready. Begora, I think that yourself ought to go to the United States Congress.

Mr. Dawson. Why so, Mr. Ready?

Andrew Ready. Bekase you have such sperit of Liberty about you. And there's too many liars and bad eggs clogging the wheels of Justice the world over!

Mr. Dawson. Now, Mr. Ready, I expect that you would want a favor if I were in Congress.

Ready. Yes, I want a great favor, and that's that you'd niver consent to an alliance with Johnny Ball.

Dawson. Why so, Mr. Ready?

Andrew Ready. God betwain us and harum. Don't you know we had to whip England before and the many fights and privations we had before we gained the Battle of Independence?

George Sears. True for you, Mr. Ready, but surely you were not in the battle?

Andrew Ready. I was not, but I suppose that apart of me heart was there.

Dawson. How do you explain that, Mr. Ready, since you were not born then?

Andrew Ready. Well, no; but me Grand Uncle—God rise his soul—was in that battle from first to last.

George Sears. But, Mr. Ready, you had no part in it?

Andrew Ready. Young man, if we all look behind us and see the material we are made of, sure! it's no lie for me to say that me heart—a good piece of it—was in the Battle of Independence, bekase me Grand Uncle was there.

Dawson. Ha! ha! That's too thin, Ready.

Ready. Excuse me, av you plase, but I think it was very thick—I came from me Grand Uncle, and that settles it.

Dawson. Say, Ready, what's that you told me once about the Priest and the Red Coat?

Andrew Ready. Faix, I'll tell yees. It was this wise: A clergyman was going the way for himself upon a foine young steed; he met an officer who stopped him. Says the officer to him; It is very quare entirely that you, a Clergyman, and very inconsfstent that you should be riding such a foine horse. Why so, says the Priest; who has a better right to ride a good horse than meself? Arra, then, says the officer, do you belave in the Scriptures? To be sure I do, said the Priest. Well, says the officer, we read in the Bible that Christ and his Apostles rode upon asses. Yes, indade, you are right, says the Priest, but a big change has taken place since then. What's that, says the officer? I'll tell you, says the Priest, of late years the Clergy cannot get asses to ride upon bekase the Gevirment is making officers out of all the asses. The officer immediately left and didn't bother the priest any more.

(All laugh ha! ha! ha!)

Dawson. Jasper, come here and sing and dance a little for our friends.

Jasper. Yes, massa, I'll do the best I can if dey won't laugh at me. (Jasper sings and dances.)

Prof. Barret. Well, Mr. Dawson, we have had a nice time and thank you very much.

George Sears. Yes, we must be going now.

Desdemona. I am sorry that you are leaving us so soon.

George Sears. Good bye, Mr. and Mrs. Dawson; good bye, Mr. Ready; good bye, Miss Dawson. We have had a pleasant time and it is with reluctance that I say farewell to you and the great State of Missouri.

Mr. and Mrs. Dawson and Desdemona. Good bye.

Jasper, Good bye, folks, I wish you all good luck.

Curtain.

ACT II.—SCENE I.

Mining Camp—George Sears met by the men on his way to the Camp—They demand more wages or threaten to quit his employ.

Sears (to men). Jack Deluerty, where are you and the men going from the mine?

Deluerty. We thought of giving up Elkhorn for good.

Sears. What! You are not going to desert me like that?

Deluerty. We thought of that.

Sears. Why?

Deluerty. Simply because there is nothing in it for you and the men.

Sears. How so! Do you not get your wages?

Deluerty. To be sure we do. But what will that amount to when you become swamped?

Sears. Jack, that's a concern of mine, and as long as you get your wages and fair treatment I beg of you and the men to return to work.

Deluerty (to men), He is a white man and treats us right. What say you? Let's go back to work.

All. So we will; so we will!

Sears. What is my small capital without the help of the brawny muscles of the miners? Patience and perseverance, I hope with God's help and the men's toil to establish a better name for the Elkhorn.

[Goes into office. Time keeper, Tom Moore, arranging fire.]

Sears. I see, Tom, that you have a good fire. It will help to cheer us up this frosty morning.

Tom Moore. Yes, Mr. Sears; but what do you think of the men quitting work? They all took their tools and left.

Sears (taking off his coat and hanging it on wall) Yes, I met Deluerty and the men out there. But they have returned to work and are in the shaft by this time.

[Noise abroad.]

Tom. Yes, I hear them going down the shaft. You seem to be troubled, Mr. Sears?

Sears. I cannot well divine that yet. Jack said they were afraid the mine would not pan out, and I suppose he thought they might get left.

Tom. How is that?

Sears. We'll, they thought that I might not be able to pay them.

Tom. That would be a bad thing, Mr. Sears.

Sears. Yes, indeed it would. Say, Tom, do you remember what the ore assays now?

Tom. I believe that it assays forty-five dollars to the ton.

Sears. I don't believe it assays quite that much. Get out the chart, please, while I read my mail, (Reads letters, examines papers, etc. Tom Moore takes the chart from drawer and hangs it on the wall.)

Tom. I will go out to the shaft and take the men's time now.

Sears. All right, Tom. [Exit Tom carrying time book. After reading mail Mr. Sears examines the chart showing the various stratas and the registered amount assayed every twenty-five feet.]

Sears. The Elkhorn will be all right yet.

[Deluerty enters office, followed by Tom Moore.]

Deluerty. What are we to do with that pump?

Sears. What pump?

Deluerty. The Buckeye pump. It seems not to be able to do the work and the men are in the water, almost to their knees and cannot stand it.

Sears. I don't want them to stand it. During the first strike I had the other pump repaired and it is all right. Tell the new engineer to hitch on to the Clevinger.

Deluerty. Indeed, I will, but it's better for yourself to give me a note to that effect; it will save a few curses.

Sears. Does Mesick swear? Tell me, Deluerty.

Deluerty. Never mind, Sears. We have the best engineer in the mountains, and when he'll tackle on to the Clevinger we will have the best pump in the Rockies. I wish I could say the same of the mine.

Sears. Now, what is the matter with the mine? I wish you wouldn't be throwing cold water on our pet like that.

Deluerty. By faykes! we need not do that, she has plenty of water and to spare. I believe the fresh mountain water would be more profitable than all the ore you'd get out of her. If you could only run the water into St. Louis it would be such a delicacy over the Big Muddy that the silk stocking folks would give you a fortune for it.

Sears. Deluerty, come here. (Deluerty arises and goes to high desk, where Sears is standing.) Say, what will you take to keep your mouth shut?

Deluerty. (In astonishment looks at him and says:) Why, man alive; you can't stop my mouth, or any other man's.

Sears. You don't quite understand me. You wouldn't like men to go about saying that your friend was a bad man, would you?

Deluerty. No, indeed; I wouldn't.

Sears. Now, understand once for all that it is very unpleasant for me to hear the Elkhorn spoken ill of, and that by my own men.

Deluerty. Begora, I don't blame you. She is your property.

Sears. Yes, and further more she has a good reputation on the market.

Deluerty. She has! has she?

Sears. I am well pleased with the Elkhorn—what need any one else care?

Deluerty. That's your business to be sure, but pardon me if I doubt in her stability.

Sears. You are my foreman and upon you I rely for my success.

Deluerty. Faith I can't help the mine if she plays out or blows up. Do you understand?

Sears. I understand very well. But listen. My capital is invested in that slice of the mountain, and if you talk about her and belittle her to every one you meet she may lose her reputation—go down in the market and ruin me forever.

Deluerty. God forbid that we should be the cause of that.

Sears. Stop talking about my Elkhorn then. I tell you what I am determined to do——

Deluerty. Whatever it is we'll carry it out if we can.

Sears. I will raise your wages from one hundred to one

hundred and fifty dollars per month, and I'll raise the men's wages 20 per cent. What do you think of that?

Deluerty. That's very good, if you can keep it up.

Sears. Then I will have an order posted up forbidding gambling on or off .duty—under penalty of being discharged forthwith. Foreman, I wish you to aid me to carry this out.

Deluerty. I'll do it to the best of my ability.

[Puts up order on wall.]

Deluerty, It's dinner time now.

[Sears goes to Hotel for dinner, the foreman and time-keeper eat in the office.]

OFFICE.	GRIEVANCES.
ELKHORN MINE ASSAY FOR STRATA.	ORDER No 3.
	All Grievances must be settled at the office. No gambling allowed, on or off duty. By order of Superintendent DELUERTY.

Tom Moore. Say, Deluerty, you have a mountain on your hands, haven't you?

Deluerty. What do you mean, Tom?

Tom. I mean what I say, that the mine is a mountain on your hands.

Deluerty. Not at all, Tom. You are mistaken. The mine is no mountain upon me nor upon anybody else.

Tom. Oh, I mean to say that it is a great bother and worry to keep things in good running order.

Deluerty. Oh, there is nothing in this world without some bother. Things cannot run smooth all the time,

Tom. Why not?.

Deluerty. Well, I'll tell you, young man. Suppose there is a railroad—the best in the world—with steel rails, good oak ties and No. 1 ballast. The cars are finely made and finished for comfort and ease. The officers and men from the section hands up to the Superintendent and President, are all well balanced and experienced men. Suppose Jack Lowney, one of the best engineers that ever pulled the throttle, ran the express on that road; mind you, before Jack goes out he always examines his pet, the engine, and only when all is right will he consent to pull the throttle. Now, after all this care and painstaking, Jack had once a terrible accident befall his train. As he was nearing Boston, coming around a curve, three cars were ditched and fifteen people killed, besides many wounded, and Jack had his leg broken.

Tom. What was the cause of the accident?

Deluerty. It was caused by the breaking of an axle of one of the coaches. Moreover, when the axle was examined it was discovered that within the center of the axle there was a vacuum that could not be discovered before and this rendered the axle weak, and when the strain of the curves came upon it a crash was the result. Here was an unavoidable accident for which no one was to blame.

Tom, That's singular,

Deluerty! Not at all, young man. This may happen every day, especially when we have men to deal with who have vacuums in their heads.

Tom. I believe you are right.

Deluerty. I am an old chap and have seen a thing or too. Let me tell you, when you have educated men to deal with —men who understand their business, especially when the right men are in the right place—everything moves along smoothly.

Tom. I believe you hit the nail on the head, old boy.

Deluerty. Yes, but when you have canary birds for men and superintendents something, yes, everything, goes wrong.

[George Sears enters.]

Sears. Deluerty, be sure and keep your eye occasionally

on the engineer. He is a good old man and tender hearted; but a nap may come over him. See that the mine is dry, perfectly dry, so that the miners may do justice to themselves and the work.

Deluerty. I shall attend to it.

Sears. After quitting time have the blacksmith overhaul the hoisting apparatus.

Deluerty. Please give me an order for the smith and I'll see that he does it.

[George Sears writes the order and gives it to the foreman.]   (Exit Deluerty.)

Sears. Tom, take these letters to the postoffice and bring me the mail.   [Exit Tom Moore.]

ACT II.—SCENE 2.

Mining camp, concluded—George Sears fills his pipe and smokes— Enter Mr. Gills, mining-stocks dealer.

Sears. Come in, Mr. Giles; take a seat.   (Giles sits down.)

Mr. Giles. Mr. Sears, I didn't think that you smoked.

Sears. It is seldom that I smoke, but I have a severe cold, and smoke to warm myself.

Giles. Queen Ann and whisky is the compound for a cold.

Sears. I never indulge in either because they make my head swim.

Giles. You are hoarse and should take something.

Sears. I believe I'll drop down and see the doctor.

Giles. By the way, how is the Elkhorn?

Sears. Very well, very well, indeed.

Giles. I understand that you have raised the men's wages, and of course this means a streak of luck and new finds.

Sears'. We have been doing as well as could be expected. Since our new machinery has been placed and a good, sober industrious set of hands employed we are going down and into the mountain further.

Giles. I suppose that you will strike it rich then?

Sears. I cannot say, but hope to. At any rate we expect to turn out more of the yellow metal and have a better lode.

Giles, I am pleased to inform you that the Elkhorn has gone up in the market. Her quotations to-day are greater than they have ever been.

Sears. I am glad of that, and shall always endeavor to keep her reputation good before the world. If money and work will develop her stores we shall bestow it upon her.

Giles. That's right, young man, she is your property, and your efforts to develop her is praiseworthy.

Sears. I thank you, Mr. Giles, for the compliment. ·

Giles. Mr. Sears, as I am in the business of mining stocks, I thought that I would drop over to tell you that I have an Eastern customer, who desires to buy your property.

Sears. What! buy the Elkhorn!

Giles. Yes. He offers $300,000.00. Will you take it?

Sears. I did not buy to sell and think if there be much of the yellow metal below I might as well have it as anyone.

Giles. True for you, Mr. Sears; but shold it not pan out as you expect it, the Elkhorn stocks would go down and you'd be a ruined man.

Sears. I must take my chances as to that.

Giles. You may do as you please, Mr. Sears. I presume that I can buy other Cripple Creek mines for my Eastern customer. However, I should like to see you do well and would pity you if the mine would prove a failure.

Sears. I thank you, Mr. Giles, for your interest in my behalf. My all is in this mine, and I could not afford a failure very well. Say, Giles, with your years of experience, what would you do if you were in my place?

Giles. With my experience and I the owner of Elkhorn, and with rather limited means I should do like the man who was offered a good price for his race horse. Sell the horse before the race came off.

Sears. Hang it, Mr. Giles, the mine is doing very well, and I hate to give up my pet. As cash down, however, is a surer thing I tell you what I will do; make the price $450,-000.00 and we'll call it a deal.

Giles. I cannot give that amount, but will wire my correspondent that the mine is doing very well and the owner will not take less than $450,000.00 for the Elkhorn.

Sears. All right, Mr. Giles.

Giles. Good day. [Exit Giles.

Tom. Mr. Sears, the pay roll is made out and the men will be here soon for their pay.

Sears. I will pay at the shaft to-day; take your book along and I will give the men their checks as they come up

[Exit Sears and Tom.]

(View them at shaft. Book-keeper reads

Jack Billings,	$24,	Sears gives check.
Chris Stein,	18,	" " "
Frank Dillon,	24,	" " "
John White,	24,	" " "
Fred Burrell,	26,	" " "
Harry Crane,	26,	" " "
William Long,	26,	" " "
Frank O'Brien,	26,	" " "
George Little,	24,	Take only 2 or 3 men
Jim Sanders,	24,	come up from below
Charles Dacey,	24,	" " "
Deluerty,	37.50,	" " "
Tom Moore,	25,	" " ")

Sears. Dacey, what have you in that bucket?

Dacey. I have some choice ore, which the foreman bade me bring up for your inspection.

Sears. Deluerty, take the ore to the office; I'll be there directly. Here is the key to the office.

[Talks to book-keeper. Scene closes.]

Deluerty goes to office and meets Giles—Unlocks door and goes in.

Giles. Where is Mr. Sears?

Deluerty. Sit down, Mr. Giles; he will be here directly. [Deluerty arranges the ore in silence.]

(Enter Sears and the book-keeper.)

Sears. Well, Mr. Giles, this is a cheerful day.

Giles. Yes, it is. It seems to be pay day, and I presume that it is cheerful for the men?

Sears. Yes, indeed it is; and they deserve all they get.

Giles. I understand that you pay the highest wages of

all the diggins.

Sears. I don't know as to that, but I pay the men what I think proper recompense for their labor.

Giles. That's right, Mr. Sears.

Sears. Then we have such good, sober, industrious men; and they steal no ore.

Giles. I am glad to hear that.

Sears. I expect that I have two or three thousand dollars' worth of fine ore specimens picked up by the men and brought to me.

Giles. That argues well for the men's honesty. By the way, Sears, I have good news from the East.

Seare. Mr. Giles, just look at this rich specimen sent up from the mine this morning.

Giles. Ah! indeed! (takes the specimen.) It is very beautiful. What will you take for this?

Sears. If you are making a collection, take it along.

Giles. Whenever, I can get a nice specimen, I take it to Denver to my wife; she has a nice cabinet, I shall accept it, and label it from Elkhorn, Cripple Creek. I thank you, Mr. Sears.

Sears. That's all right.

Giles. I have had advices by telegram about that deal we were talking about.

Sears. Well, what news have you?

Giles. I am empowered to give you for the Elkhorn the nice sum of $420,000.00.

Sears. I thank you, Mr. Giles, but cannot part with my pet for that amount.

Giles. Have you considered the matter well, young man?

Sears. Yes, I thought over it some, and was sorry that I had offered it for $450,000.00.

Giles. (Jumps up and walks about the room.) Upon my word, Mr. Sears, I want to do justice for my correspondents as well as for you. However, if you have capital enough can see your way through and can stand a failure, should it come, it is for you to say.

Sears. I will not back down from the price I made you, but certainly will not take a copper less.

Giles   Well, Sears, put it there.   You are a man of your word.   I will take it at $450,000 and close the deal.   Here is my certified check for $10,000, the balance I'll pay you to-morrow at the bank.

Sears.   Just as you say, Giles.

Giles.   Well, all right, Mr. Sears.   You will continue in charge of the Elkhorn till the first of the month and have all the output for your trouble.

Sears.   I'll do so with the greatest of pleasure.

Giles.   Moreover, say nothing about the deal till I make it public in the papers.

Sears.   Well, I shall keep mum about the matter and go along as though nothing transpired.

Giles.   Now, Mr. Sears, I think that I have done well for my correspondents in the East and I am firmly convinced too that the sale is the best thing for you and hope that you are perfectly satisfied and that success may surround your pathway through life.

Sears.   Thank you! Thank you, Mr. Giles.

[*Curtain.*]

ACT II.—SCENE 3.

Mount Calme Hospital—View of the sick—Mr. Perkins with broken leg—Sergt. Procter, a sick soldier— Geo. Sears has pneumonia.

Sister Clare.   (Placing a bandage on the soldier's head.) Have good courage and you will get over this.

Sergeant.   Do you think so? Tell me, Sister, will I get entirely well?

Sister.   Certainly. But you must have patience and courage.

Sergeant.   I am glad.   I'll try.   (Knock is heard at the door.) (The Sister opens the door.) (The Doctor comes in.)

Dr. Gross.   Good morning, Sister.

Sister.   Good morning, Doctor.

Dr. Gross.   How are the patients to-day?

Sister.   They are as well as could be expected, Doctor. All are improving.

Dr. Gross.   How is our man with the broken limb?

Sister.   He is getting on well, but perhaps he took a little too much exercise yesterday.

Doctor.   Has Mr. Sears sat up any to-day?

Sister.   No, Doctor.   He seems a little despondent to-
day.

Doctor.   What is the cause of his despondency?

Sister.   I cannot say, Doctor.

Doctor.   I hope he is not getting a relapse.

Sister.   I think his business affairs trouble him.

Doctor.   Has he had any visitors?

Sister.   Only a few.

Doctor.   Maybe he has talked too much or read too much.

Sister.   He has read nothing but some letters, and he has
talked but little.   (They enter sick room.)

Sister.   Mr. Perkins, here is the doctor.

Perkins.   I am glad you have come.   I had a little fever
and pain in my limb last night.   (Exit Sister.)

Doctor.   What is the feeling there now?

Perkins.   It is quiet to-day, but I haven't walked any
yet.   I am a little afraid to.

Doctor.   Yes, you had better be a little shy of walking
much for a few days.

Doctor.   Did you walk some yesterday?

Perkins.   Yes, I went out on the porch—in the yard and
about the place.

Doctor.   What did your nurse say about it?

Perkins.   She told me that I was doing too much; but
the day was beautiful and it was new life for me to get
about.   (Sister returns.)

Doctor.   Let me examine your limb.   (Examines.)   It is
all right—only the exercise was too much yesterday.   Be
careful to-day and don't go out any.

(Sears is propped up in bed.)

Doctor.   Good morning, Mr. Sears.

Sears.   Good morning, Doctor.

Doctor.   How are you feeling?

Sears.   Pretty well, Doctor.

Doctor.   (Feels pulse and looks at watch.)   Your pulse is
good,   Places small thermometer in mouth.   Doctor in

meantime reads his notes, takes out thermometer and marks temperature in book.)   Do you feel as well as you did yesterday morning?

Sears.   I am not so well.

Doctor.   Did you take medicine regularly?

Sears.   I did, Doctor.

Doctor.   Sister, did he take much nourishmedt yesterday?

Sister.   He only took his beef tea a few times.

Doctor.   Sister, Mr. Sears is on the road to health, but I'd like to account for this little change.

Sister.   I don't know why he should be weaker.

Doctor.   You did not attempt to sit up yesterday, did you?

Sears.   No, Doctor, I did not.

Doctor.   I am confident that something must have caused you pain.   Now please tell me, Mr. Sears, what you believe to be the matter.   As I am treating you I think it necessary for me to know.

Sears.   I received rather painful news yesterday.

Doctor.   Was it the death of a friend?

Sears.   No! not exactly, doctor.

Doctor.   Well, then, you should not trouble yourself nor permit any sadness to come over you.

Sears.   I know that but could not help it.

Doctor.   It might aggravate your sickness.   Moreover, you are a Christian and know as well as I can tell you, Mr Sears, that everyone has crosses to bear in this world.

Sears.   Yes, that's so, Doctor.

Doctor.   Your present necessity of getting well should be paramount in your mind.   Please try and be cheerfultoday.

Sears.   I will try, Doctor.

Doctor.   (Writes prescription and gives it to the sister.) Have him take this every three hours and read some good book to him.

Sister.   I will, Doctor.

Doctor.   Take your medicine and be cheerful, Mr. Sears. Good bye.

(Doctor visits soldier.)

Doctor.   Well, Sergeant, how do you feel this morning?

Sergt. Morris.   I feel pretty well now, but I had a hard time of it last night.

Doctor.   What was the trouble?

Sergeant.   I had quite a battle such as I never had before in my life.

Doctor.   Indeed!   I presume that you must have been dreaming.

Sister.   The night watch said that the Sergeant was talking vigorously in his sleep.

Doctor.   You don't say?   Well, Sergeant, what was the battle you were fighting?

Sergeant.   I thought that I was in the midst of the fray in Manila Bay and a shell exploded in our midst, taking the top of my head off.

Doctor.   That was rather severe.

Sergeant.   I think that the medicine must have caused this terrific battle.

Doctor.   Yes, I presume that was the cause but you feel much better to-day.   How is your head?

Sergeant.   Clear as a whistle, thank the Lord.

Doctor.   The amunition we gave him, Sister, put the enemy to flight.

Sister.   It was the proper thing, Doctor.

Doctor.   To be sure it was.

Sergeant.   I am satisfied with the result.

Doctor.   (Feels pulse, looks at patient's tongue and writes prescription.)   Some light nutritious food and a quiet rest with little medicine will set you all right in a few days.

Sergeant.   I thank you, Doctor   .

Doctor.   After noon, Sergeant, I would advise a little nap and afterwards if you feel like it read a pleasant story. Sister Clare will get you a book from the library.

Sergeant.   That's just what I would like.

Doctor.   I think the war is over now and you'll have no more battles.   Good morning, Sergeant.   Good morning Sister.

Sister.   Good morning, Doctor.

[*Curtain.*]

ACT III.—SCENE 1.

The Dawson house—Mrs. Dawson sewing—Miss Desdemona returns from taking music lesson—Has her violin music.

Mrs. Dawson. Well, daughter, how did you succeed with your lesson to-day?

Desdemona. Very well indeed, mother. ❧

Mrs. Dawson. What do you think of the violin by this time?

Desdemona. Well, it is like every musical instrument. It has its peculiarities.

Mrs. Dawson. Do you like it?

Desdemona. At first, you know, I did not like it. It was only to please Father; but I am learning to love the violin.

Mrs. Dawson. Your father will feel mighty proud of that. He thinks the violin the best of all instruments.

(Jasper, colored servant, brings in a letter for Desdemona and a paper for Mrs. Dawson.) (Desdemona reads her letter.)

Mrs. Dawson (looking over at her daughter, who appears sad.) Desdemona, pray, what is the matter?

(Desdemona walks around the room.)

Mrs. Dawson (putting her arms around her daughter.) Tell me, Desdemona, what troubles you?

Desdemona. The Lord preserve him! Yes, mother, you shall always be the treasurer of my secrets.

Mrs. Dawson. What causes you to be sad?

Desdemona. Mr. Sears is down with fever, and I fear that it will go hard with him, mother.

Mrs. Dawson. Yes, I presume that it is very severe, but has he not a good nurse, Desdemona? Let me see; I will read the letter. (Mother reads letter.)

Dear Desdemona:—Since disposing of the Elkhorn mine I took a severe cold which culminated in pneumonia. Feeling that something severe was coming upon me I came to the Sisters' Hospital, where every care is bestowed upon me. I cannot liken the Sisters to anything but angels in human form. They have been a mother to me and prayed and watched at my bedside whilst my life was in peril. The Doctor, too, has been attentive and, thank God, my life has been spared. I am able to sit up in bed and write you. Unless a relapse or something unforseen happens I am in a fair way to recover. If you hear from my sister don't mention my sickness, lest mother would venture out to see me. The journey and change at this season of the year would be too much for her. Give my regards to your parents, and for yourself accept my best esteem. Pray for me, darling, and may God bless you. Yours truly, GEORGE.

Mrs. Dawson. Now, my dear, it might be worse, and as he is well cared for let us hope and pray that Mr. Sears will get better.

Desdemona. Yes, mother, we will pray that he will soon be restored to health and strength.

Mrs. Dawson. Yes, daughter; we have every reason to hope so. (Enter Mr. Dawson.)

Mr. Dawson. Well, I have struck a good bargain to-day —ha! ha!—'deed I did. You don't catch this old chap a napping.

Mrs. Dawson. Well, what bargain did you make to-day?

Dawson. Why I sold my Brush Creek farm, and that at a good price, too.

Mrs. Dawson. Who bought it?

Dawson. Why don't you ask what I got for it?

Mrs. Dawson. Well, what price did you receive for it?

Dawson. Seventy-two dollars an acre. It is a good price; yet it's a good bargain.

Desdemona. Who bought it, pa?

Dawson. Call me dad and I'll tell you.

Desdemona. Why, pa is nicer than dad!

Dawson. No it ain't either, by George!

Desdemona. Well, now, dad, who bought the upper place?

Dawson. Well, Desdie—now I'll tell you. It was old Uncle Aleck. Ye see it jined his farm on the west, and he wanted it mighty bad and he paid my price for it.

Mrs. Dawson. Did he pay you the money down?

Dawson. You bet your bottom dollar he'll do it. He gave me one thousand dollars down and will pay balance when his lawyer passes on the abstract.

Mrs. Dawson. There is just two hundred acres in that

farm, and at $72 per acre it will fetch just $14,400. How is that?

Mrs. Dawson. That is a good sum.

Dawson. Well, Julia, I feel good over that trade and am going to give you and Desdie some change to go a shopping. Opens pocket-book.) Here, Julia, is a hundred dollars. Desdie, my dear one, come here; here is another hundred for you, daughter. (Desdemona comes forward and receives the bills from her father, who sees a letter sticking out of her bosom.)

Desdemona. I thank you very much, father.

Dawson. By the way, Desdie, what is that you've got there?

Desdemona. It is a piece of writing, father.

Dawson. Let me see it, daughter.

Desdemona. Why, dad, you don't want to see this?

Dawson. Why not, daughter?

Desdemona. Because——(puts finger to her mouth)— well, yes—because it is my letter.

Dawson. Well, let me see it. Tain't a love letter, is it?

Desdemona. It's from a dear friend, father.

Dawson. Your friend shonld be my friend, Desdie, Let me see who it is!

Desdemona (reluctantly hands letter to Dawson.) There, now, father, you won't read it, will you?

Dawson (puts on his spectacles and takes the letter out of the envelope and reads; "My dear Desdemona"—looks over at his daughter surprisingly.) Why, Desdie, who is this calling you his dear Desdemona?

Desdemona (looking at her mother.) He is a friend, father.

Dawson (reads on). "Pray for me, darling, and may God bless you. Yours respectfully and truly. George Sears." Desdie, let me see, (scratching his head) is this the Kentucky dude who came to see you a few times?

Desdemonia. Yes, father; he is a Kentuckian, but is in the mountains now.

Dawson. Y-e-e-s, at Cripple Creek, too, I suppose to try his fortune, ha! ha! ha!

Desdemona. Yes, father, you remember his sister, Miss Emma, who was visiting me last summer.

Dawson. Y-e-e-s, she was a nice gal, but I say whoo! Emma, and whoo! Desdie, don't let it ever get into your head that I am a going to let you marry a miner of Cripple Creek or anywhere else.

Desdemona. But if I loved him, father?

Dawson. You must git it out of your head, Desdie. You bet you must!

Mrs. Dawson. Let us drop the subject, for she is not going to marry now, anyway.

Dawson. I know something of these love affairs. I've been there myself and know jist what I'm a talking about. (Turning to his daughter.) Do you hear me, Desdie?

Desdemona. Yes, father; give me my letter and we will call it quits for to-day.

Dawson. Y-e-e-s, and forever; you bet your bottom dollar. Here's your letter.

Desdemona. Thank you, father

Dawson. Desdie, I want yer to hear your father. Now honor bright, Jim Henry is going to be a doctor. He'll come back from Edinboro on top of his profession and I want you—the darling of my heart—to be a musician of the highest standard.

Desdemona. I am doing all I can, dad, to please you in that line.

Dawson. Yes, gal, you seem to be. But let me tell you that any person that's in love can never git there.

Desdemona. That may be with the men folks, but not with the ladies.

Dawson. Dar, you git me, Desdie. I is sure its the case with the men folks but how can I tell about the women? Call your mother.   [Exit Desdie.]

Dawson. I don't know what's got into this girl's head anyhow.

(Mrs. Dawson and Desdemona enter.)

Mrs. Dawson. What is the matter?

Dawson. Say, wife, I's been a telling Desdie that I want her to get to the top round of the ladder in music and told her she could never get there and be in love at the same time.

Mrs. Dawson.   Why so?

Dawson.   Kase the Good Book says so.

Desdemona.   I never heard the like; where does the Bible say it, father?

Dawson.   I jist don't know the chapter nor the verse, but it says that we can't serve two masters at the same time.

Mrs. Dawson.   Yes, the Scripture says that no *man* can serve two masters.

Dawson.   We won't quarrel about it, but you always heard that we must not have too many irons in the fire, 'cause some of them might get burned.

Desdemona.   I shall do my best, father, to climb the music ladder.

Dawson.   Say, wife, do you know what I heard in town?

Mrs. Dawson.   I cannot say.

Desdemona.   What is it, father?

Dawson.   They tell me that Prof. Barret and his family are making arrangementts to go to Europe.

Mrs. Dawson.   What will daughter do for a teacher then?

Dawson.   I'll tell you what she will do.

Desdemona.   He did not say anything about going when I was there.

Dawson.   No; he is a man that says little about his business affairs, but I know that he sold his property and intends starting away in a short time.

Desdemona.   Do you tell me?

Dawson.   Yes, I do tell you, and what is more, I'm a going to git up and git out of this country myself.

Mrs. Dawson.   What's a coming over you, anyway, Stephen?

Dawson.   Missouri is too slow, and I am thinking of selling out and going abroad.

Mrs. Dawson.   For what! husband?

Dawson.   For business and pleasure.   Yes, I am determined to do it.   (He rises.)

Desdemona.   My dear father, hear me, if you please Surely you are not going to sell our homestead?   This beautiful place, where you have spent so many happy years of your life—where you have always been blessed with peace and plenty. O, do but consider this spot—the birthplace of your children—the home of your family as the most sacred place on earth. Next to the church, father, it has been the vestibule of Heaven. O! Do not, I beg of you, think of parting with it forever. Consider dear mother, think of brother and look upon me as your dutiful child. Do not, I beg of you, break our hearts!

Dawson. Well, daughter, rather than break your hearts and divorce you entirely from my old sweetheart, Missouri, I shall retain our home place.

Desdemona. I thank you, father, thank you.

[Exit Mrs. Dawson and Desdemona.]

(Enter Jasper with Mr. Blake.)

Mr. Blake. I hope that I do not intrude.

Dawson. Not at all, friend Blake, you are always welcome to the Dawson home.

Blake. I understand that you are going to the World's Fair at Paris and dropped down to see if you will rent your home place.

Dawson. I expect I will.

(Enter Mrs. Dawson and Desdemona.)

Mrs. Dawson. I am glad to see you, Mr. Blake.

Desdemona. How do you do, Mr. Blake?

Blake. I am well, thank you. In case, Mr. Dawson, you will rent the home place I have a man who will take care of everything and give you a fair price for the rent.

Dawson. Who is the man?

Blake. It is George Weber.

Dawson. Old Fred Weber's son?

Blake. Yes, sir, he is the man.

Dawson. I thought he owned a farm of his own.

Blake. He does. It is rented and he can't get it for two years.

Dawson. Well, I'll rent him my home place as long as he wants it—I know he will take care of it.

Mrs. Dawson and Desdemona. Why! We are not going to leave, are we?

Dawson. Yes, my dear ones, we are going to leave for a while, at least. Did I not tell you so before?

Mrs. Dawson. Yes, but we thought that you were only joking.

Dawson. I was always in earnest about the matter.

Blake. Now, folks, I must leave you as I have considerable business to attend to. Mr. Dawson, shall I draw up the contract for the rent?

Dawson. Yes, Mr. Blake, you may do so and I will only ask Mr. Weber three dollars an acre.

Blake. I think that amount very reasonable and am confident that it will be satisfactory to Mr. Weber, and you no doubt will be pleased with your tenant.

Dawson. I am so glad that our home will be in such good hands. Tell him that we will give him possession inside of two weeks.

Blake. Mrs. Dawson and Miss Desdem ona, I must corgratulate you on the prospects of a pleasant tour. Mr. Dawson, give me your hand. (Shake hands.) I must admire you on the afternoon of your life to be so level-headed and considerate for yourself and family to take such needed rest and recreation. I hope that we shall meet at the great World's Fair. Good morning.

Dawson. Good morning and God bless you, Mr. Blake. [Exit Blake.] Now, wife and daughter, what do you think of me? Am I such a great old fool after all?

Mrs. Dawson. No indeed, husband!

Desdemona. I am so glad, dad, that we are not to part with our dear old home.

Dawson. I don't blame you for that, daughter. This has been the home of your childhood and many happy days we have all spent here together. Miss Louri was my first sweetheart and your mother was my next.

Mrs. Dawson. Steve, what is that you say?

Dawson. Julia, dear, you are and have always been the apple of my eye. (He goes over to her and kisses her.)

Mrs. Dawson. What do you mean?

Dawson. I mean, Julia, that you and Miss Louri are my

sweethearts. We have labored and worked well together and now you and Desdie and I are going to have a grand time at the World's Fair.

(Enter Jasper and Mr. Ready.)

Ready. The top of the morning to yees. (All rise and shake hands with Mr. Ready. All say good morning, Mr Ready.)

Ready. Well, Miss Desdemona, you are a bright girl— God bless you. Av I was a young man I'd set me cap for you, and when I'd pop the question you would say yes! Wouldn't you, now. Tell me a fra?

Desdemona. I don't know, Mr. Ready.

Dawson. Julia, don't that remind you when you and I was a courting.

Mrs. Dawson. I don't remember.

Dawson. Y-e-e-s, indeed, you remember what a mighty bashful gander I was.

Mrs. Dawson. Yes, and what a goose I was.

Ready. Indade, I believe you were more like ducks and drakes—ha! ha! ha!

Dawson. Sit down, Mr. Ready. (Sits down.) Did you hear the news, my friend?

Ready. What news do you mane, sir?

Dawson. My family and I are going to the Old World.

Ready. Don't tell me.

Dawson. Y-e-e-s, we are going.

Ready. Be the powers the papers are full of such things, and I hope you are not going to lave us.

Dawson. Y-e-e-s we are going sure pop.

Desdemona. Mr. Ready, we are going across the water to the World's Fair at Paris.

Ready. Oh? I see now! Indeed that's a foine place.

Dawson. Well, Mr. Ready, I do wish you were going with us to Paris.

Ready. Faith and I'm going to onld Ireland this summer, plase God.

(Enter Jasper.)

Jasper. Law bless you, massa, what's a-goin' to be done wid dis nigger if you are all goin' to leave?

Dawson. Don't mind, Jasper. If we don't take you along we'll provide for you.

Jasper. Lord bless you, massa. I is Jasper Dawson all over.

Ready. Begorry, ave yees don't take him wid yees, send the Darkey over to my house and he may stay with us.

Desdemona. Just think of it! This may be the last time that we meet in old Carroll county for many a day.

Dawson. Never mind, Desdie, we shall all meet here again.

Desdemona. May God grant it, father.

Ready. I do wish you folks would get a peep at the Emerald Isle before you come back to America.

Dawson. Why do you want us to go to Ireland?

Ready. Becase it is the foinest country in the world.

Desdemona. Do you think, Mr. Ready, that Ireland is finer than the United States?

Ready. Of course, Miss, the United States is greater in extent of territory and while the Stars and Stripes is the grandest flag in the world and this Govermint is the best under the sun, still I belave that the scenery of Ireland is the foinest on the globe.

Mrs. Dawson. I heard that Killarney lakes and scenery could not be surpassed anywhere.

Dawson. Julia, if that's so we must visit Ireland.

Ready. I wish you could take a sail on the Bay of Dublin and see the Wicklow mountains. You'd never forget it in all your life.

Dawson. Why, my wife knows a song called "The Bay of Dublin."

Ready. Mussha, it is a long time since I heard that song, and a foine one it is. Oh, I'd like to hear that song.

Dawson. Mrs. Dawson, jist please sing that song for the gentleman.

Mrs. Dawson. Certainly, I will. I am not much of a singer, but will do the best I can. Miss Barret, will you please play the chords for me?

Miss Barret. If you have the music I can do so with the greatest of pleasure. (Miss Barret plays piano and Mrs. Dawson sings "The Bay of Dublin." All admire and clap.)

[*Curtain.*]

ACT IV.—SCENE I.

Paris—The Dawsons at Hotel Continental Rue de Rivoli, Paris.

Mrs. Dawson.   Desdemona, what do you think of Paris?

Desdemona.   I am delighted, mother, with Paris.   I think it the Capital of the world.   It is lively and beautiful.

Mrs. Dawson.   What about the language and the people?

Desdemona.   The language I don't understand, but think it sounds sweetly.   The French people speak with so many gestures and are so very polite.

Mrs. Dawson.   I believe our morning ride is the most beautiful of all my life.

Desdemona,   Indeed, mother, I think the Champs Elys'ees and the Bois de Boulogne the most beautiful places that I have ever seen.

(Enter Jasper with tray.)

Jasper.   Here, ladies, is de sham pane.   Look out; it pop!

Desdemona.   Here, Jasper, open it.

Jasper.   I'se 'fraid.   (He opens it.)

(Enter Mr. Dawson and Count la Far.)

Dawson.   Ladies, I am glad that you are enjoying yourselves.

Mrs. Dawson.   We were so thirsty Desdemona and I thought that we would have some champagne.

Count la Far.   Indeed, and that is very nice.   How did you enjoy that ride papa and I did arrange for you?

Desdemona.   We enjoyed it very much, Count La Far.

Count.   What is your opinion now of France—I mean Paris in particular?

Desdemona.   We are perfectly delighted with Paris, your capital city.

Dawson.   Wife and daughter, it was really grand to-day. Tell me are not the people very kind and polite everywhere?

Mrs. Dawson and Desdemona.   Indeed, they are very kind.

Count.   Now, ladies, to tell you the truth I vas in London, Edinburg and many other places that were very fine, but I never found such beauty and life and pleasure anywhere as in my native Paris.

Desdemona.   While Paris is beautiful there is no place

that has such charms for me as America—especially my native State, Missouri.

Count LaFar and Dawson. Why so, Miss Desdemona?

Desdemona. I will confess that art has sway here in Paris, and while she is at the zenith of beauty in that respect, Missouri has youth and wealth of natural beauty which is simply grand.

Dawson. I am so enchanted with Paris that I believe I will cast my lot here.

Mrs. Dawson. This is a good place to stay until you get tired.

Desdemona. It must cost something to keep up this gay way of living in the Capital.

Count. Indeed, for rich people that's very little. Then persons can live a more retired life if they wish.

Dawson. It becomes people who want a good time and see life. Paris, I think, is the gayest of all European cities.

(All drink champagne.)

Count (holding up his glass.) Viva la Belle France.

Desdemona. Viva la Madamoiselle Missouri.

Mrs. Dawson. Here is to our friends.

Dawson. Here is to our noble selves. (They drink.)

Count The very drink and food of France cannot be excelled anwhere in the world.

Dawson, Wife, come this way. I wish to consult you about some matters and will let the young folk talk over the beauties of Nature and those next to their hearts.

[Exeunt Mr. and Mrs. Dawson.]

Desdemona. I think the French kitchen is one of the best. I am satisfied, however, with American cooking.

Count. Pardon me, Miss Dawson, but do you not enjoy the dishes of la Belle France?

Desdemona. I do, indeed.

Count. What is your objection, then?

Desdemona. I have offered no objection, but merely said that our American cooking suited me best.

Count. Since the French kitchen is counted the best, would you not be pleased to always enjoy the French dishes with me?

Desdemona. I will say that the French cooking is very nice, but would prefer American cooking. ,

Count. Pray, I beseech you, Miss Dawson, tell me the reason.

Desdemona. I prefer American dishes because I am accustomed to them. Secondly, because they are easier digested.

Count. I see you are afraid of indigestion. But I can assure you that the French food is better in this climate. Now, tell me, how you like the people here.

Desdemona. I like them very much indeed. They are very polite.

Count (rising.) Shake hands, Ma Belle Missouri. (She puts her hand in his and he draws her to his side.)

Desdemona. What do you mean?

Count. I mean to thank you in true French style for your kind esteem.

Desdemona. How is that, Count LaFar? Is there a special way for thanking people?

Count. Yes! Madamoiselle Dawson, there is a special way. I will show it to you. Give me your hand. (She gives her hand.) Look me in the eyes. (He kisses her on the forehead.) I thank you very much.

Desdemona. What have you done?

Count. I simply placed my lips upon your handsome brow, from which came your esteem for me.

Desdemona. You amaze me. You are so very unnecessarily polite. Words would be sufficient to convey one's thoughts and esteem.

Count. But my dear Miss Dawson, I must congratulate you Belle America. My heart goes out to all that is good and noble. I cannot express to you my sentiments on this occasion.

Desdemona. Why so?

Count. Pardon me, Miss Dawson. It is impossible for me to express sufficiently my esteem for you.

Desdemona. I perceive your people make a good many unnecessary gestures they ought to save themselves.

Count. Since you are so kind as to express esteem for us

I would like to return the compliment in true French style.

Desdemona. I will be better pleased with the American style.

Count. I must then simply say to you, Miss Dawson, that I love you.

Desdemona. I am thankful that your people and Americans respect and esteem each other.

Count. I am so glad that you American beauties love us.

Desdemona. Yes, we love you at a respectful distance.

Count. I like very much that American song——

Desdemona. Marching through Georgia?

Count. I could understand better if you would sing it for me.

Desdemona. I am not in a singing mood to-day, but will ask cousin Nance to sing it for you. (Goes for Miss Nance and she enters.)

Count. I am glad you are so kind to come and sing for me.

Miss Nance. I will be pleased to do so.

Count. We like foreign airs and American music is very fine.

Miss Nance. I wifl try to please you. (Sings.)

Desdemona. Well, Count, how do you like the song?

Count. I am delighted and hope to have the pleasure of hearing you some day.

Desdemona. When I am in singing mood I will favor you with a song.

Count. Now, ladies, I must leave you. I am sorry, but business of importance demands my attention. Good evening, my dear ladies.

Desdemona. Good bye, Count.

[*Curtain.*]

ACT IV.—SCENE 2.

Hotel Continental, Paris—Desdemona writing at table.

(Enter Mr. Dawson.)

Dawson. Well, Desdie, how do you get along with your music?

Desdemona. Father, since I have heard that Concert at the Grand Opera House, I am convinced that your pet is about the finest instrument. I believe that a master hand should call forth its music.

Dawson. Well, how are you making it with the Count? I mean Count la Far?

Desdemona. What do you mean, father?

Dawson. I mean can you love him?

Desdemona. Love him as God's creature—-yes, but not otherwise.

Dawson. Is he not polite and very kind?

Desdemona. Yes, he is crazy, nonsense.

Dawson. I understand, too, thet he is very wealthy.

Desdemona. Pshaw! father, why do you want to get rid of me in a foreign country?

Dawson. I love you, Desdie, and want you to marry a gentleman of wealth and honor.   .

Desdemona. I prefer to choose an American, and as for wealth and honor, I don't believe the Count has much. I am of the opinion that he wants to marry for wealth and American honor.

Dawson. The Count is very wealthy, and tells me he loves you.

Desdemona. Pshaw! father; don't let him pull the wool over your eyes. I think La Far is a broken-down Count, and wants our money.

(Enter Mrs. Dawson.)

Mrs. Dawson. Desdie, I wish that you would not have anything to do with that La Far. He is no Count at all.

Dawson. Why so, wife?

Mrs. Dawson- A lady next door says that he has spent all he has and lives off his widowed sister.

Desdemona. Indeed, mother?

Mrs. Dawson, So I have heard from the lady.

Dawson Well, if it's a fact, he is a scoundrel. I'll find out from the Assessor. I'll just go to the office and have the clerk telephone the Assessor.   [Exit Dawson.]

Desdemona. Mother, did you hear that Count la Far was living with or off his widow sister?

Mrs. Dawson. Yes, daughter; he is living with his sister,

and is dependent on her for his support.

Desdemona. Is he then no Count?

Mrs. Dawson. Oh! he is a Count, and, no doubt, of noble family, but he has squandered his fortune, and makes no use whatever of his ability or education.

Desdemona. And this is the gentleman, Monsieur La Count, which my father desires me to wed? No! I shall never marry him.

Mrs. Dawson (embracing her daughter). Yes, you are right, Desdemona.

(Enter Dawson with hand full of letters.)

Dawson, Desdie, here is a letter from your Kentucky dude, I believe. Julia, dear, here is a letter from Carrollton, Missouri.

Desdemona. Father, please don't call my friend a dude, which he is not. Mr. George Sears is a gentleman in every sense of the word.

Mrs. Dawson. My own dear Stephen Dawson.

Dawson. What is it, Julia?

Mrs. Dawson. My dear old sweetheart. You always loved your wife and children. Tell us about your new-found friend, Count LaFar. Is it so that you are going to stay in Paris and engage in business with him?

Dawson. Who told you so?

Mrs. Dawson. Your actions and words of praise.

Dawson. It is not so. I have all the business I want taking care of you and Desdie.

Desdemona. Oh, father, what have you learned about the Count! Has the Assessor told you of all the great property he owns?

Dawson. Confound the Count. I don't believe he is a Count at all. At any rate I found out from the Taxman that LaFar was only a gentleman in poverty.

Desdemona. Indeed, father! And where is his wealth gone? Are you still anxious that I should marry this gentleman?

Dawson. I did not say that you should marry him. I only said that he loved you.

Desdemona. Father, I believe that it is your money he loved.

Dawson. Hang him; he lied to me and I believe that he is a scoundrel.

Mrs. Dawson. LaFar may not be a scoundrel, but we must beware of such new-made friends.

Dawson. I must confess that I like Paris very much, but I don't understand French and am disgusted with their grinning politeness.

Mrs. Dawson. The French Capital is indeed a great city and I have no doubt at all but that many of her citizens are noble-hearted people.

Desdemona. Yes, indeed mother, you are right. Some of the brightest intellects of the world were citizens of France.

Mrs. Dawson. Yes, and the nation has always acted kindly towards our dear America.

Desdemona. Yes, mother; when our country was struggling for liberty, Gen. LaFayette gave his fortune and his sword to America.

Dawson. Well, Desdie, you may stay and marry the No-Count if you want to, but your mother and I are going to leave the country.

Desdemona. God forbid, father, that I should ever marry a man that is No-Count.

Dawson. Hold on there, Desdie, I meant no offense, but surely you would not marry that dude, who sent that letter?

Mrs. Dawson. My dear Steve, don't tantalize Desdie so.

Dawson (placing his arms around his daughter.) Cheer up, Desdie, the right man has not come along yet—when he does, we shall place no obstacle in the way.

Mrs. Dawson. Steve, did you get any letters?

Dawson. Yes, I got one from Andrew Ready. He is in Dublin, Ireland.

Mrs. Dawson. What does he say?

Dawson. He says the country is delightful, and wants us to meet him in Dublin, and he will show us the beauty spots of Erin.

Mrs. Dawson. Shall we go?

Dawson. To be sure we will, but first we must go to London, where they speak plain English, and have Desdie finish her musical education.

Mrs. Dawson. Right here in Paris is the best place for that, and a few more weeks will finish her, I think.

Dawson. Well, as you say, Julia, but as there are too many Counts here for me, I want to leave as soon as possible for London.

Mrs. Dawson. We have seen the World's Fair, many museums and works of art, and, if you wish, we will leave Paris any time you name.

Dawson. Suppose, then, we leave Saturday and we will reach London Sunday morning.

Mrs. Dawson. All right! this will give us three days more—ample time to see all that we haven't seen.

Dawson. After lunch we will go out to the Hotel des Invalides. Desdie, I will go for the carriage; get ready before lunch. [Exit Dawson.]

Mrs. Dawson. Now, daughter, your father says that we must be ready to leave for London next Saturday.

Desdemona. Ah, me! that's too bad, mother, for George will be here next week—Wednesday—and how can I get to see him?

Mrs. Dawson. Have you received a letter from Mr. Sears?

Desdemona. Yes, mother; here it is. (Pulling letter out of her pocket.)

Mrs. Dawson. Read it for me, Desdie.

(Desdemona opens letter and reads).

Nazareth, Ky., July 12, 1900.

My Dear Desdemona:—Learning from Mr. Blake that the Dawson family had left for the World's Fair, I did not have the pleasure, which I anticipated, of meeting you at Carrollton Heights. I did not stop there at all, but came on here to visit mother and the folks. I have been here just two weeks, and have had a delightful time with relatives and friends of my youth. There was only one thing lacking to make my joy complete, and that was the presence of my dearest friend, Miss Dawson. However, it may be all for the best. I have made arrangements with Mr. Blake, who is now my financial agent, to meet me in New York, and, after attending to some business matters there, we will both sail for Paris. I hope to reach there about the 5th of August. Pray that we may have a safe and speedy voyage. I found mother and sister and all the folks well. They join me in kindest regards to you and your parents. I hope that you are enjoying the Great World's Fair, and expect to meet you all at the American exhibit. I cannot say what hotel we shall stop at, but will register at the New York Herald office, where you can address me. Yours with esteem,

GEORGE SEARS.

Mrs. Dawson. Well, I declare—Mr. Sears and Mr. Blake are both coming to the World's Fair, and how glad we should be to meet them.

Desdemona. Yes, indeed, mother; can you imagine how I would like to see Mr. Sears?

Mrs. Dawson. Daughter, I appreciate your position very much, and am at a loss to know how we can arrange a meeting with those kind friends.

Desdemona. Cannot father go on to London and secure quarters for us at some good hotel?—and we could go on afterwards.

Mrs. Dawson. Yes, that is possible, but I don't like to have your father travel alone.

Desdemona. Why so, mother?

Mrs. Dawson. Well, he has never traveled alone much, and now during World's Fair year there are so many rascals and some Counts abroad.

Desdemona. You are right, mother, but how shall we meet our friends?

Mrs. Dawson How would you suggest, Desdemona?

Desdemona. Well, mother, father seems to be determined on going to London on Saturday, and lest he might run up against some more Counts, I think that it is better for us to go.

Mrs. Dawson. But what about the gentlemen?

Desdemona. Well, mother, we can have them come over to London and see us.

Mrs. Dawson. That is a capital idea and the best way for all concerned. Leave a letter at the Herald office for George.

Desdemona.   Capital idea, mother, capital idea.

[*Curtain.*]

ACT V.—SCENE I.

London—Grand Hotel, Trafalgar Square—Mrs. Dawson and Desdemona.

Desdemona.   Mother, London reminds me somewhat of New York.

Mrs. Dawson.   Yes, daughter, but it appears more old and quaint.   How does it compare with Paris in your estimation?

Desdemona.   From what I have seen, mother, Paris is far ahead of London.

Mrs. Dawson.   London is one of the greatest business cities in the world.   What strikes you to be contrast with America?

Desdemona.   There is more art and a better class of it in Europe, generally, than in America.

Mrs. Dawson.   You are right as regards art, my dear; these old countries are far in advance of us.   What is keeping your father?   (Enter Dawson.)

Desdemona.   Here comes father, now.

Mrs. Dawson.   Well, Count Dawson, we are glad that you have come.

Dawson.   Please, now, don't call me that again.

Desdemona.   Why, father, don't you like that name?

Dawson.   No, I don't, it is too Frenchy for me.

Desdemona.   Why, mon paire, it is a distinction of honor.

Dawson.   Please, your honor, we are now in the British Dominion, and I prefer to be called Lord than anything else.

Mrs. Dawson.   Lord Dawson, you have keen perceptions. Now tell us what you think of London and Londoners?

Dawson.   Mrs. Lord Julia, you amaze me.   Have you not eyes and ears of your own?

Mrs. Dawson.   We have; but we want your judgment on the matter.

Dawson.   You remind me of the Henglish people; you want what you have not.   Your own opinion is not enough for you, but you want mine, too.

Desdemona.   What do you mean, father?

Dawson.   You bewilder me, child.   Call me Lord, lest I might forget it.

Desdemona.   Well, Lord Dawson, may it please your honor to speak out the knowledge and inform us regarding the general character of this great noble race with whom our country may form an alliance?

Dawson.   To be frank, I hope that shall never occur.

Desdemona.   May I ask you, Lord, to speak the answer to my question about the people?

Dawson.   History tells us that away back the English people were a noble and hardy race, but with wealth they became haughty, and now the tendency is to look down upon the lowly.

Mrs. Dawson.   I believe the English people are noble and generous-hearted.

Dawson.   No doubt you will find as whole-souled and generous people in England as anywhere upon the globe.

Desdemona.   Why then, father, do you speak so disparagingly of the nation?

Dawson.   You must understand Lord Dawson, my daughter

Desdemona.   How so?   Please explain, my Lord and father.

Dawson.   A Monarchial Government is too close and selfish; whereas a Republic is the contrary.

Desdemona.   I see, father, that a Republic is like a large family and has a tendency to broaden the views of its members and make them more charitable and God-like.

Mrs. Dawson.   True, for you, Desdemona; the Charter of American Liberty teaches the Golden Rule of loving one another and working for the welfare of the masses.

Desdemona.   Viva la America.

Dawson.   Long live the glorious Republic of America.

Mrs. Dawson and Desdemona.   Amen! So may it be.

(Dawson arises, takes off his coat and ties an American flag around his waist.)

Desdemona.   Father, that is a nice flag—why tie it around your waist?

Dawson.   Because it makes me strong.   It reminds me of the suffering of my forefathers.   (Taking off the flag.)   Wife and daughter, behold these stripes of red!   They·tell us of the blood of martyrs, and the sufferings of our soldiers in the great Battle of Independence.   These stripes run side by side—parallel with each other—and they indicate the unanimity of action of the braves, who fought the battles of Young America.   These Stars are the Stars of Liberty—bestowed by Almighty God upon the young, struggling American nation.

Mrs. Dawson and Desdemona.   "Hail, Columbia! the gem of the ocean, the land of the free and the home of the brave."

Dawson.   Three cheers for the Red, White and Blue!— Three cheers for the United States and you   (All give three cheers.)   (Enter Jasper.)

Jasper,   Mr. Dawson, your carriage is ready.

Dawson.   I am going out to find our friend—·your old professor—Mr. Barret.   I understand that he is located somewhere in the city.

Desdemona.   Oh! father, I would like to go to him.   He is so kind, and then he is such a good teacher.

Dawson.   It is quite warm.   Stay where you are until I find Prof. Barret's place.

Desdemona.   (Puts arms around her father and kisses him.)   Father, you are so kind.

Mrs. Dawson.   Dear Lord, Steve, I hope that you will find Prof. Barret.

Desdemona.   Father, beware of the Counts.

Dawson.   I shall do so.   Take care of yourselves while I am gone.   [Exit Dawson.]

Mrs. Dawson.   Daughter, how lovely, after all, our trip has been.

Desdemona.   Yes, mother, it has been an object lesson and many things we have learned in these old countries.

Mrs. Dawson.   Yes, Desdemona, travel broadens our intellect and makes us see more and more the blessings of liberty which we enjoy at home.

Desdemona.   Yes, indeed!   We, moreover, perceive the great arts which flourish on the Continent.

Mrs. Dawson. How happy our American citizens would be if they would devote more time to the sciences, fine arts and travel and give less time to corn and cattle.

Desdemona. You are so considerate, mother. I am glad that you see things in their proper light.

Mrs. Dawson. I have learned so much on this trip, and am thankful to God and Lord Stephen for the pleasure of this journey abroad.

Desdemona. Indeed, we should be thankful. How grand is this Earth! How lovely is God to make it for us! Yes, mother, this life is worth living that we may enjoy it and so act towards the Creator and our fellow-man that we be deemed worthy to enjoy the bliss of Eternity.

(Enter Jasper with card.)

Mrs. Dawson (taking card, reads). George Sears,
Cripple Creek, Colo.

Desdemona. What is it, mother? Who is it?

Mrs. Dawson. Mr. Sears must be in the hotel—this is his card.

Desdemona. Oh! you don't say. What! George Sears here? (Takes the card and kisses it.)

Jasper. Yes, mum; the gentleman is down in the parlor.

Mrs. Dawson. Desdemona, you had better have him come up.

Desdemona. Jasper, wait a moment. Mother, are we dressed for company?

Mrs. Dawson. Daughter, we are all right—have our American friend come up immediately.

Desdemona. Jasper, show Mr. Sears up. [Exit Jasper.] (Desdemona looks in the mirror.)

Mrs. Dawson. Our friend cannot have been longer than a week at the World's Fair.

Desdemona. I hardly think so. I am sure that he received my letter at the Herald office.

Mrs. Dawson. To be sure he has.

Desdemona. How kind in him to come on so shortly.

(Enter Jasper and George Sears.)

Jasper. Missus, here is Master Sears from the United States.

Mrs. Dawson.   We are so glad that you have come, Mr. Sears.   (Shakes hands.)

George Sears,   I am also very glad, indeed.

Desdemona.   Why, Mr. Sears; we are delighted to see you! Jasper, take Mr. Sears' hat and cane.

Jasper.   Yes, mum, you bet I will.   He is a gentleman from the United States.

Mrs. Dawson.   We presumed that you were coming, Mr. Sears, but did not anticipate such an early visit.

Sears.   I would have liked to have seen more of Paris and the World's Fair, but was afraid that I might miss you, if I tarried longer.

Desdemona.   You are so kind, George.   Mother and I had planned to meet you at the Colorado exhibit in the World's Fair building.

Mrs. Dawson.   Our arrangements, however, were made, and we were obliged to depart for England.

Sears.   Yes, I presumed so.

Desdemona.   Did you have a good voyage across the ocean?

Sears.   Yes, we had a delightful voyage, except on Friday afternoon—there was a severe storm which lasted about an hour.

Mrs. Dawson.   Were the passengers frightened?

Sears.   I should say they were.   All were calling upon God's mercy to protect them.   Even I heard two gentlemen who professed no faith call upon God to save them.

Desdemona.   Mr. Sears, I think the boundless ocean, especially in a storm, makes one think of Eternity.

Sears.   Yes, it is a good place to make excellent resolutions for the living of better lives.

Desdemona.   George, you no doubt were delighted with Paris and the World's Fair?

Sears.   Mr. Blake and myself traveled continually and I must say that Paris is the finest city that I have ever seen.

Mrs. Dawson.   Will Mr. Blake remain long on the Continent?

Sears.   Yes, I presume he will remain a month or so.   He is a nice gentleman, thoroughly reliable and I expect to engage him in my business as long as he is willing to remain.

Desdemona. I think Mr. Blake an excellent gentleman.
Where is he now?

Sears. He has gone to see Professor Barret and his sister.

Mrs. Dawson. Why, Mr. Dawson left for there just before you came.

Sears. Mr. Blake has business with Mr. Dawson and expects to return here and see him.

Mrs. Dawson. I am glad, indeed. Mr. Dawson will be delighted to meet him.

Desdemona. What a contrast between the Old World and the New, Mr. Sears!

Sears. In point of vastness the American continent seems greater. Its mountains are higher, and in fact our farms and business are on a more elaborate scale. Europe, however, has the advantage of age and experience over us. Paris alone, I verily believe, has more fine architecture than all America A view from the Notre Dame Cathedral presents a scene that is simply grand.

Desdemona George, did you notice the carvings over the central entrance of the Cathedral?

Sears. Yes, my dear, it is a carving of the last judgment; it was pointed out to us by the guide. It is the finest thing of the kind that I have ever seen. It made me ask myself the question, am I ready for judgment?

Mrs. Dawson. What was the answer, Mr. Sears?

Sears. Pardon me, Mrs. Dawson, you question me too closely, but I thought that I was not ready.

Desdemona. What else of interest did you see in Paris, Mr. Sears?

Sears. Besides the Cathedral, there are many interesting churches. We visited a few palaces. We visited the palace of the Tuileries, that was the home of Louis XVIII., Charles X., Louis Philippe and Napoleon III. The President of the Republic of France lives now in the Palace de Leysee. We also saw the Palace du Luxembourg, where the Senate of the Republic holds their sessions. We visited many fine parks and gardens, the most famous promenade in Paris—and one of the finest in the world—the Champs Elysees. We stood in the Caucarde Square, in the center of which is the Luxor Obelisk, given to Louis Philippe by the Pasha of Egypt.

Desdemona. Did you see the great Triumphal Arch, George?

Sears. Yes, My dear. It is an imposing piece of architecture that cost about two millions of dollars. There are many fine drives and cemeteries but we had no time to visit them. The Hotel Des Invalides, or Home for the Old Soldiers, and the Gilded Dome attracted our attention. It is an immense building and has a church attached in which is the tomb of Napoleon I. In a chapel on the left is the tomb of Jerome Bonaparte and on the right is the Sarcophagus of Joseph Bonaparte, once King of Spain. We visited the Opera House, which covers about three acres.

Desdemona. George, did you see the Colossal Statue in the Colorado exhibit?

Sears. I saw it, but did not admire it.

Mrs. Dawson. Why did you not admire that beautiful statue?

Sears. Because I was looking for something greater.

Desdemona. And what was it, George?

Sears. Shall I tell you?

Desdemona. To be sure, George.

Sears. It was an animated statue that I wished to see.

Mrs. Dawson. Indeed, Mr. Sears, and what do you call that statue you sought so much?

Sears. It was Desdemona.

Desdemona. Ha! ha! ha! and do you know what I have been longing to see?

Sears. No, my dear, I cannot guess.

Desdemona. It is a work of art—made by the grandest of all Architects.

Sears. Please name it.

Desdemona (rising). Well, it is a gentleman from America.

Sears (rising and taking Desdemona's hand). Thank heaven that we have found each other.

[*Curtain.*]

ACT V.—SCENE 2.

*Grand Hotel, London—Sir Albert Murdock's courtship repulsed—
Miss Desdemona's engagement to Mr. George Sears becomes known
—Rev. Mark Austin arrives from the United States, and with
Dawson's consent, will unite Desdemona and Mr. Sears in wed-
lock—Mrs. Dawson, Desdemona and Sir Albert Murdock.*

Mrs. Dawson. You need not appeal to me, Sir Albert.
My daughter is old enough to speak for herself in a matter
of such importance.

Sir Albert. Ah, yes, indeed; but would you not give
your daughter good advice?

Mrs. Dawson. Yes, to be sure I would, and will whenever she needs it.

Sir Albert. Now, what advice would you give Miss Desdemona on this occasion?

Mrs. Dawson. This is not the proper time to give advice
—neither has she asked me.

Desdemona. No, mother, I don't think it necessary in
the present crisis. Your heart is ever with your child and,
never fear, I understand its gentle promptings. Sir Albert,
you must not consider that my mother would interfere with
my love affairs.

Sir Albert. I thought it was her duty to guide and direct you in such affairs.

Desdemona. No doubt, Sir Albert, the counsel and advice of our mother should always be directed for our temporal and eternal welfare.

Sir Albert. Why, then, should it not be imparted in the
present instance?

Desdemona. My mother's advice and counsel have often
been sought and given.

Sir Albert. I very much admire your mother and as I am
in love with you, I only sought her influence in my behalf.
If you could see my heart you would understand me, and I
hope acquiesce, to become my partner for life.

Desdemona. The promptings of the human heart should
be compatible with the will of the Creator.

Sir Alber. Believe me when I tell you that our Creator

has prompted my heart to admire that which is grand and noble. Ah, yes, if you would only acquiesce and reciprocate my love I believe that it would be recorded in heaven.

Desdemona. True, for you, Sir Albert, it would be recorded, yet not compatible with the will of God.

Sir Albert. Why not, I pray you?

Desdemona. Because I love another.

Sir Albert. Let me ask you to consider well your first engagement. May it not be premature or misplaced?

Desdemona. I think not, Sir Albert.

Sir Albert. I fear that you may not have considered properly the nature of the engagement and hence it would not be binding upon you.

Desdemona. I have considered the matter and after mature deliberation I am perfectly satisfied with my engagement.

Sir Albert. Miss Dawson, you must not consider for a moment that I seek aught else but that which is just and right.

Desdemona. I hope not, Sir Albert.

Sir Albert. We all have our likes and dislikes and when I met you at the Barret School of Music, my heart went out to you. When I found that you were educated and a lady of good parentage, I said to myself and before God, "That is a pure creature and one worthy of companionship."

Desdemona. Indeed! Sir Albert.

Sir Albert. Yes, Miss Dawson, I believe not the doctrine of predestination, but I do believe that like seeks like and it should not be otherwise.

Desdemona. Your ideas are correct, Sir Albert.

Sir Albert. I believe, therefore, that I am traveling in the right direction when I seek your companionship in holy wedlock.

Desdemona. Indeed! Sir Albert.

Sir Albert. Yes, Miss Desdemona, could you look down into my heart, you would see there the worthy motives which prompt me to ask your consent to our alliance.

Desdemona. While I do not question your motives I believe not in a foreign alliance.

Sir Albert. Pray, why not?

Desdemona. Simply because it is not necessary. Now we are friends and independent of each other. Let us remain so.

Sir Albert. But if we cannot effect this holy union what will become of my heart?

Desdemona. It will become more sagacious and seek a more congenial union.

Sir Albert Do you believe it possible?

Desdemona. Most assuredly, Sir Albert. I am an American and you are English; our ideas are different and we could not agree.

Sir Albert. But we could learn.

Desdemona. Sir Albert, pardon me, but your school days and mine are over. We are moulded differently and hence seek a friend that can be more compatible, I pray you.

Sir Albert. Pardon me, Miss Dawson, can I not yet look upon you as a friend?

Desdemona. Yes, Sir Albert. I admire your frankness and you may consider me your friend, but nothing more. (Turns away and again facing him.) May God direct you in the true path.

Sir Albert. I thank you, Miss Dawson, from the depths of my soul. Good bye for the present. (Shake hands.) I hope that we shall meet again.

Desdemona. I hope so. Good bye. [Exit Sir Albert]

Mrs. Dawson. Desdemona, what do you think now of the young Lord?

Desdemona. Mother, you ask me what I think of Sir Albert; I will tell you. I consider him a nice gentleman and think that he will make a good suitor for some excellent young lady.

Mrs. Dawson. I admire your perseverance in rejecting his advances. It is good in you to do so, Desdemona.

Desdemona. Considering my engagement with Mr. Sears, it would be wrong to encourage Sir Albert.

Mrs. Dawson. By such encouragement many girls cause trouble and even sometimes murder.

Desdemona. How wisely the Church prohibits such foolish nonsense.

Mrs. Dawson. Certainly a promise of marriage rightly and maturely made is binding in conscience.

(Enter Mr. Dawson and Jasper.)

Jasper. Law md! Desdeemona, what did you wid the Lord?

Desdemona. Shut up, Jasper. I have nothing to do with the Lord but obey His holy will.

Jasper. I don't mean the Lord Massa in Heaven, but that gentleman who was here. He went away a-crying to hisself.

Desdemona. Jasper, you will mind your own business.

Jasper. Why, I's got nobody to love me.

Desdemona. Yes, Jasper, you must love the Lord thy God above all things and your neighbor as yourself.

Jasper. What's you going to do when your neighbor won't speak to you and some tothers feel so big as the Lord hisself. What you going to do then, Miss Desdie?

Desdemona. Never mind such people; let them alone. Only pray for them.

Jasper. I don't like to pray for such folks. Let them pray for hisself.

Desdemona. Yes, Jasper, but if you want the Lord to forgive you your sins you must forgive your neighbor.

Jasper. If dat's so I gis I haf to do it; but don't like to.

Desdemona. Here, Jasper, get a pitcher of water.

[Exit and brings it back.] (Mr. Dawson has lit his pipe and is talking to Mrs. Dawson.)

Dawson. Yes, London is a great big overgrown city. By the way, Desdie, my child, have you made it all right with the Lord?

Desdemona. Whom do you mean, father?

Dawson. Why, I mean Lord Murdock, to be sure.

Desdemona. Indeed, father, I am surpised at you— thinking that your daughter would marry anyone who is imbued with imperialistic ideas. No, father; I want no one to be Lord over me, but God himself.

Dawson (jumps up surprised). Mother, what does all this mean?

Mrs. Dawson. Stephen, my dear, do you not know that

Desdemona has a sweetheart this long time—the past three years at any rate?

Dawson. No, I did not know it, and I don't want to know it.

Desdemona. Yes, father, you remember that I gave you, as you requested, my sweetheart's letter to read.

Dawson. You have reference to that Kentucky dude—sit down. (Refills his pipe.) Do you think for a moment that I could allow you—my own Desdemona, my darling child—to marry that young sycophant? Not at all.

Desdemona. My dear father, I appreciate your love for me, and rest assured that I shall never wed a flatterer, nor a scape-goat. If I cannot marry a Christian gentleman I shall not wed at all.

Dawson. If that be the case, then why not consider the character, the standing and the qualifications of Lord Murdock?

Desdemona. Simply: because he is an imperialist and arrogates to himself a title which should belong to God alone. I believe in a Republic whose citizens subscribe to the Constitution, the great magna charter of Liberty.

Dawson. Barring that, Desdie, cannot an Englishman be a cultured gentleman?

Desdemona. Father, certainly he can. However, you would not want your daughter Lorded over by any man.

Dawson. Give me your hands, Desdie. As God is our witness to night I would slay the man—brute that would injure you.

Desdemona. I am glad, father, that you understand the spirit and principles of true liberty.

Dawson. To be sure I do.

Mrs. Dawson. Stephen, dear, why not let your daughter then be governed by the principles of Christian liberty and let her choose her own husband! (Desdemona sobs.)

Dawson. But, Julia, it is our duty—mine in particular—to look after her temporal welfare.

Mrs. Dawson. Yes, and her spiritual welfare too and above all else.

Dawson. Let us reason about this matter. Come now,

Julia; come, Desdemona. Hear me. As God is in Heaven I will nothing but the welfare of my daughter.

Desdemona. Yes, father, mother and I believe that. But we are looking beyond the vale of this world.

Dawson. That is eminently proper, Desdie, and it is for that reason that I would like you to wed, and will have you marry Lord Murdock, a wealthy, nice gentleman.

Desdemona. Father, with all due respect for you, I cannot marry Sir Albert.

Dawson. Is he not a nice gentleman, and with plenty of wealth to care for you?

Desdemona. I scorn his wealth.

Dawson. Do you tell me that you will not marry him?

Desdemona. I have said it, father.

Dawson. (Rising and dashing his pipe to pieces upon floor). By the eternal! I shall know the reason! I have looked hard for your welfare—given you an education and come to Europe for your benefit, and now that I have succeeded in obtaining a good man—an honorable gentleman and wealthy, who is willing to become your husband— you scorn me from the depths of your heart.

Desdemona. Nay, father!

Dawson. I tell you and your mother that I shall stand this no longer. (He takes drink of water.)

Mrs. Dawson. Stephen, I am surprised at you. You will kill your daughter.

Dawson. Kill nothing.

Desdemona. Hear, me father.

Dawson. No! You have said too much. I will not.

Mrs. Dawson. Stephen, I beg of you to be calm!

Desdemona. O, father, hear me, your child. No one loves you greater than I.

Dawson. Well, what is it? Speak out.

Desdemona. Be patient with me and I will tell you all. No secrets will I keep back from you, for you are my own dear father.

Dawson. What is it then? Be quick!

Desdemona. My father, to you whom God has given me as my protector and guardian. To you I owe respect and obedience in all things compatible with the will of Heaven. Before I can leave the sacred spot that we call Home—before I can leave you and my dear mother—before I can transfer my love and allegiance from you I must be sure that he who takes your place in the affections of my heart must be one whom I can call husband in the true sense of the word—a Christian gentleman. Wealth and worldly honor cannot buy the affections of my heart.

Dawson. What do you seek for in a husband, Desdemona?

Desdemona. Besides the qualifications, father, dictated by taste—such as beauty of form and age—there are others far more necessary.

Dawson. Pray, what do you consider the proper qualifications for a husband?

Desdemona. The virtues which I seek in a husband, besides Divine Faith, are Prudence, Justice, Fortitude and Temperance.

Dawson. Lord Murdock possesses these and far more. Be obedient to me and look upon him as one worthy of your hand.

Desdemona. No, father, it is impossible. I cannot obey you in this.

Dawson. But, Desdie, I say to you that I have authority and you must obey.

Mrs. Dawson. Stephen Dawson, I beseech you to consider the rights of your daughter and coerce her no longer.

Dawson. Away, woman! do I not know my business? Desdemona, come, tell me are you ready to obey me or not?

Desdemona. My father, there is our Father in heaven whom I must obey first, above all else in the world. (kneels) O, God, look down upon me in this hour of trial, grant that I may do nothing but what is compatible with Thy Holy will. Father, remember, father, my soul and yours—their salvation is at stake.

Dawson. Am I not laboring to that end when I seek for you an honorable husband?

Desdemona Yes, father; but you know that I have a right to accept or reject him. Moreover, I am engaged to an honorable gentleman, whom you cannot but admire.

L. of C.

(Enter Jasper with cards on tray.)

Dawson. Give me those, Jasper. (Reads names). Show the gentlemen in, Jasper.

Mrs. Dawson. Husband, you ought to become acquainted with the gentleman whom your daughter likes.

Dawson. Where is he? In Kentucky, I suppose.

(Enter Jasper with Mr. Blake and George Sears.)

Syl Blake. I am glad to find you within. Allow me to introduce Mr. George, of Colorado. Mr. George, this is my friend, Mr. Dawson.

Dawson. I am glad to meet Americans.

Mrs. Dawson. Mr. Blake, I am glad that you have come.

Blake. This is my friend, Mr. George, of Colorado.

Mrs. Dawson. I am pleased to meet Mr. George.

Dawson. Mr. George, allow me to introduce you to my daughter. Miss Desdemona, this is Mr. George, of Colorado.

Desdemona. I am so happy to meet you, sir! Do you like London?

Mr. George. At present I like it very much. I don't believe that I would like to live here.

Dawson. This is a great, busy, bustling city.

Mr. George. I prefer America and American ways of doing business.

Blake. But it is nice to visit and see how our neighbors get along.

Mr. George. That's what we have come for.

Dawson. You have been in Paris, haven't you?

Mr. George. Yes, Mr. Dawson, but I have not seen very much of it. We expect to return there before leaving on our homeward tour.

Dawson. Say, Mr. Blake, I hope that you will give us a wedding this Fall.

Blake. Yes, perhaps before we go back.

Dawson. We may have a wedding in our family afore we leave London.

Blake. Ah, indeed! Miss Desdemona, I presume, has met some gallant she admires?

Desdemona. No, indeed, Mr. Blake, father is joking.

Dawson. There is no joking about it, an English Lord is

deeply in love with her. All she has to say is yes, and we'll have one of the grandest weddings.

George. Would you, Mr. Dawson, extend Mr. Blake and myself an invitation?

Dawson. To be sure I will, gentlemen.

Blake. ' Do you hear this, Miss Desdemona?

Desdemona. Indeed, I do, Mr. Blake. Nothing would give me more pleasure than to have you both at my wedding

Blake. Give me your hand, Miss Desdemona. That's a bargain. Remember it, please.

Desdemona. Certainly, I will!

Dawson. I do hope that we will have a wedding in London.

Desdemona. Mother, Mr. Blake contemplates a wedding in London, and father is anxious to give me away, too, so we may have a double wedding, you see.

Mrs. Dawson. I think one wedding at a time might be enough. Mr. Blake, I think you are acquainted with a nice lady, Miss Celia Barret.

Blake. Yes, she is a nice lady and a dear friend of mine, Mrs. Dawson. Please put in a good word for me there.

Mrs. Dawson. I don't think it necessary, because she admires you. I think your chances are good.

Mr. George (rising.) I must leave this good company now.

Dawson. Don't be in a hurry, Mr. George. I would like to hear something about the great mountains and mines of Colorado.

George. I should be glad to do so, but am obliged to go to my hotel and get some important letters. Moreover, I expect on this afternoon steamer a dear old friend of mine.

Dawson. I am sorry that you are obliged to go.

George. I will now bid you good evening.

Dawson. Good evening.

Desdemona (gets hat and cane). We shall be happy to see you again soon, Mr. George.

George. I hope so. Good evening.

Desdemona. Good evening

George. By the way, Mr. Blake, shall I look for you over to supper?

Dawson. We will be apt to keep him here for supper and talk about home folks and old times.

George. All right, Mr. Dawson; but don't let him remain out too late in London.

Mrs. Dawson. I will see that Mr. Blake gets off in time. (Desdemona throws kiss after George.)

Mrs. Dawson. That seems to be a nice gentleman.

Dawson. Look here, Mr. Blake, where did you come across this nice young man? I declare I like him.

Blake. The first time that I met him was in Carrollton. Afterwards I took a vacation and went to Colorado and by chance met him at Cripple Creek, where he owned the Elkhorn mine. We became fast friends, and I can honestly say that he is one of the finest gentlemen that I have ever seen.

Dawson. Do you tell me so! What is he doing over here, Mr. Blake?

Blake. I will tell you, and how we happen to be together. I was contemplating a visit to the World's Fair when I received a letter from Mr. George stating that he was going to Paris on business of importance and asked me to accompany him and take charge of some business for him.

Dawson. What business?

Blake. He ships ore and specimens to foreign countries and deals also in mining stocks.

Dawson. How much do you reckon he is worth?

Blake. I can't say exactly, but think that Mr. George is worth at least a million.

Dawson. That's a great deal, I declare, and he is a young man yet.

Blake. He was 24 on his last birthday.

Dawson. I am surprised—and he is so wealthy.

Blake. When Mr. Geo. Sears was 21 years of age he went to the mountains and put all his money in Cripple Creek and struck it rich. It seems to me, Mr. Dawson, that you met him at Carrollton. He was visiting the Barrets on Folger street.

Dawson. Say, Julia, it appears to me there was a young man who came to the house with the Barret family the day of our social picnic.

Mrs. Dawson. Yes, it was the day you sent over for Mr. Ready and all had a great game of croquet.

Dawson. By Jove, that's it! I remember it now. (Dawson lites his pipe.) He wanted to take Jasper away to the mountains. Desdemona, do you remember anything about this gentleman a-playing croquet that day?

Desdemona. Yes, father, I remember it very well.

Dawson. By gosh, he is a fine man!

Blake. He was just from college and very thin at the time; but Mr. Sears has developed wonderfully and is now a fine proportioned man.

Dawson. Yes, indeed! I think that he is a nice looking gentleman.

Desdemona. I am of the same opinion, father. I am glad to know that you like my Kentucky Dude.

[*Curtain.*]

ACT V.—SCENE 3.

The Barret school of music, London—Prof. Barret, Miss Celia Barret and Miss Desdemona Dawson.

Celia Barret. I must congratulate you, Miss Desdemona. (Enter Jasper).

Jasper. Massa Dawson and the Missus am a coming, and I run afore, kase I like dem music.

Desdemona. Jasper, sing something.

Jasper. Miss Desdemona, I can't sing much, you know dat.

Barret. Yes, Jasper, come and sing.

Jasper. If de professor give me fiddle, I'll sing for the ladies.

Barret. All right, Jasper; here is a violin. Be careful and don't break the strings.

Jasper. You bet I won't. Let's see—now what you have? Say quick, afore Massa comes.

Desdemona. Give us something lively, Jasper.

Jasper. Well, here goes. (He plays and sings, etc.)

(The bell rings and Jasper runs to open the door. Enter Mr. and Mrs. Dawson.

Barret. Good morning, friends of the Stars and Stripes.

How are you all to-day?   [Exit Desdemona.]

Mrs. Dawson.   We are well, I thank you.

Dawson.   Come close to me, people.   I want some information from you.   (They sit close.)   You all know how I have loved my daughter.   Say Barret, if your dad was alive he could tell you how this old fellow worked and plowed and harrowed in the Missouri Bottom 30 years ago.

Barret.   I expect he could.

(Jasper down near the door takes down a brass instrument and blows into it.)

Dawson.   Come here, Jasper; what you a-doing there?

(Jasper comes before Mr. Dawson.)

Jasper.   Why, Msssa, I was a-looking into this here brass thing and it hollered.   (All laugh.)

Dawson.   I'll make you holler if you don't stop.

Jasper.   Scuse me, Massa.   [Exit Japser, bowing]

Dawson.   Now, folks, you remember I was a-saying how hard I worked in the Missouri Bottoms when we used to get the shakes.

Barret.   Yes, Mr. Dawson.

Dawson.   I worked hard not only to get a home for myself and family, but I have strained my nerves to gain something more in order to leave my family in good circumstances when I die.

Barret.   You have done well, Mr. Dawson.

Dawson.   Yes, I have done the best I could, at any rate, and have educated my family.

Celia.   You deserve praise for it, Mr. Dawson.

Dawson.   I always wished my daughter, Desdie, to marry a Lord or someone with royal blood.

Barret.   I thought that you were more of an American.

Dawson.   You bet your bottom dollar I am an American and love my country too.

Barret.   Pray, why should you seek a Lord as a husband for your daughter?

Dawson.   Well, I'll tell you.   You see I thought Lords always had plenty of money and a good education.

Barret.   Yes, but often they are spendthrifts and tyrants.

Dawson.   Why! You don't tell me?

Barret Yes, many of them are dissipated wretches.

Dawson. Well, I declare!

Mrs. Dawson. He saw some of that himself in Paris.

Dawson. Professor, tell me, do you know this Mr George who is over here with Mr. Blake?

Barret. Yes, Mr. Dawson, I know him very well, indeed. He is a cousin of our family, and an educated gentleman.

Dawson. Now, professor, I want to know the honest truth about him. How old is he, and what business is he at?

Barret. When we left Kentucky, he was a young boy going to school. Afterwards he went to college, and graduated when he was twenty-one—that's just three years ago.

Dawson, What has Mr. George been a doing since?

Barret He has been engaged in mining.

Dawson. How came he to get a mine for himself?

Barret. Let me see—when old Mr. Sears died in Kentucky he left his family in good fix, and when George became of age he got his share and went to the mountains.

Dawson. Has he lost his money, or made a stake in the mountains?

Barret. I should say he has done well. He sold the Elkhorn mine for 450 thousand dollars—nearly a half million.

Dawson. Tell me truthfully, is he a good man? He wants Desdie, I understand, to marry him.

Barret. Allow me to say to you that of all the young men I have ever known, George Sears is one of the best.

Celia. Yes, and he will make an excellent husband for Desdemona, because he is very kind and generous. Let me show you what George brought me from Paris. (Gets present.) (Enter Desdemona.)

Dawson. Come here, Desdie. (She comes to her father.)

Desdemona. What is it, father?

Dawson. After all, Desdie, I think that your Kentucky dude has developed into a full-grown man.

Desdemona. I am glad that you think so, father.

Dawson. Notwithstanding that I wanted a man of royal blood as husband for you, I shall put no obstacle to your marrying Mr. George Sears.

Desdemona. O, father! I am so happy, and thank you

from the bottom of my heart. (Embraces her father.) (Miss Celia shows her presents.)

Mrs. Dawson.   They are very fine, indeed.   Desdemona, show what Mr. Sears brought you from United States.

Desdemona.   Father, look at the present which Mr. Sears has brought me.   (Mr. Dawson takes it.)

Dawson.   That's dazzling.   (All exclaim; "How beautiful; how fine it is!'')

Dawson.   Desdie, why don't you wear your present?

Desdemona.   I was afraid of you, father.   I thought you might not like it.

Dawson.   Yes, my child. you may wear it.

(Enter Jasper.)

Jasper.   Dare is a carriage down front house, and the man says, "what you want to go home?''

Dawson.   Yes, Jasper, you go down and tell him we'll be there, directly.

Jasper.   Yes, Massa; I'll do so.   [Exit Jasper.]

Dawson.   Well, Professor, we must be a-going, I reckon. Desdie, you had better come along, too.

Desdemona.   Father, I would like to remain, with your consent.   I will meet Mr. George Sears here this afternoon.

Mrs. Dawson.   Let her stay, Stephen.

Dawson.   Well, Desdie, you may stay till evening.   Be home then, of course.

Desdemona.   Yes, father, I will.

Dawson.   Good morning, all of you.   I shall never forget your kindness.

Mrs. Dawson.   Good morning.   Prof. Barret and Celia, when are you coming over?

Celia.   We will go over this evening or to-morrow.

Mrs. Dawson.   All right, Be sure and come.

[*Curtain.*]

ACT V.—SCENE 4.

The Wedding Banquet at Grand Hotel, Trafalgar Square, London —The Table is laden with the best—Prof. Barret Master of Ceremonies—Jasper and Sam Waiters—Music by Orchestra while the Guests are coming in—When all the guests are about the table Father Austin and the Bride and Groom make their appearance and take their places.

Dawson.   Father Austin, please ask the blessing.

Father Austin.   Yes, sir!   I will in the name of the father and of the Son and of the Holy Ghost, Amen.   Bless us, O Lord, and these, thy gifts, which we are about to receive from the bountiful Providence.   (All answer Amen and sit down to table).

Blake.   Well, Mr. Dawson, I must congratulate you on this American wedding.

Dawson.   Say, Blake, it will be your turn next.

Blake.   Yes, I suppose so.

Sir Albert.   Father Austin, when you left home did you expect to have a wedding?

Father Austin.   No, Sir Albert, I did not.   I merely came to London to visit my friends, the Barrets, and to get posted regarding Paris before going to the World's Fair.

Sears.   I am glad that you were agreeably surprised.

Desdemona.   Mr. Ready, how is Ireland?

Ready.   Musha, I don't know!   Ireland is all right, but the people are still suffering from the tyranny of the landlords.

Sears.   Is the scenery of Ireland as fine ss it is represented to be?

Ready.   Yes, indeed it is.   No finer country the sun shines on, but I'd never live there again.

Dawson.   Why so, Mr. Ready?

Ready,   Because there is no liberty there.   Give me our glorious Republic of America.

Father Austin.   You are right, Mr. Ready, the Stars and Stripes represent more of God's benevolence to man than all the governments of the world,

Andrew Giles. Mankind live more like one family in the United States than in any of the Old Countries.

Blake. Of course we should respect our neighbors and their governments.

Ready. To be sure, Mr. Blake, but for God's sake invite all you can to the friendly, Christian shores of America.

Sir Albert. But pray, Mr. Ready, what do you think of the Philippines and the expansion business engaged in by the United States?

Ready. The politicians and a few would-be officers and imperialists have brought that about. The majority of the people, however, are not in favor of any imperialism.

Dawson. Barring that foolish war, the Republic of the United States is the most admired the world over—her citizens are the most happy and her prosperity the greatest the world has ever seen.

Blake. True for you, friend Dawson. As long as the citizens of the United States remain faithful to the principles of the Constitution prosperity will reign—but when they depart therefrom and worship the Golden Calf, thei honor and glory shall wane.

Dawson. You are right, Mr. Blake. (Rising.) Here is to the goose that raised the quill that made the pen that wrote the Constitution.

Ready. That was a good goose. God bless her.

Lord Murdock (rising.) With your permission I will give my toast. Here's to woman, whose heart and whose soul are the light and the life of each spell we pursue; whether sunn'd at the tropics or chilled at the pole, if woman be there, there is happiness too.

Barret and others. Good! good! Mr. Blake, it's your turn now, please give us a toast.

Blake (rising.) Here's to bride and mother-in-law; here's to groom and father-in-law; here's to sister and brother-in-law; here's to friends and friends-in-law; may none of them need an attorney-at-law.

Dawson. Ha! ha! That is a good wish, indeed. Mr. Ready, please give us a toast.

Ready. Here's to the Land of the Shamrock so green;

here's to each lad and his darling Colleen; here's to the ones we love dearest and most; and may God save old Ireland! that's an Irishman's toast.

All.   Good! good! Mr. Ready, Bravo!

Father Austin.   I suppose I ought to give a toast too. Here is to America, the land of the free and the home of the brave. May the emblem of liberty, the stars and stripes, over you forever wave.

All.   Amen! amen!

Barret.   Mr. Sears, will you please favor us with a toast?

Sears.   Ladies and gentlemen.   Here is to those we love and to them that love them that love them that love those that love us.

[*Curtain.*]

FINIS.